That Happily Ever After Kinda Love 2

BY: LOVELY ANN

Table of Contents

Acknowledgments

First, I wanna give honor to God, without him, this wouldn't be possible.
To my husband, my biggest supporter, thank you, baby, for pushing me
to continue when I was struggling to get this book done. I love you, bae.
To my children Lil Eddie (Eddie iv), DeAndre (Dre), Lakiaya (Kiaya),
you three mean the world to me and remember, I'm doing this for you
and showing you that you can follow your dreams and be what you want
to be. I love the 3 of you.
Mom, you are another big supporter of mine. You done had me a
t-shirt made with my first two books on them and that showed love to
me you have bought and read both my books. I'm glad I could make
you proud I love you Ma.
Dad, thank you for showing your support. I know I can be a brat at times
but hey, that's just me.
My sister Cassandra, thank you for supporting me. We have our ups
and downs, but we always have each other's back. I love you, sis.
My brothers Ricky and Corey, I love y'all and thank you for the support.
To my girls (Lonzia, Jess, Sweets, Shae, Amanda, Theresa, and
Phylicia), that I have met while reading some of the same authors and
now we have become good friends; well, shit, we are like family really
but still I'm glad I met all of you. I love y'all ladies and thanks
for supporting me. Lonzia and Jess, thanks for pushing me to keep
writing even when I was feeling down. Y'all knew what to say to keep
me going. Shit, Sweets and Shae, y'all two and these ladies always have
me laughing with all y'all petty asses.
Finally, last but not least, Mama Diane (R.I.P). We love and miss you
every day. May you continue to rest in peace. Thank you for accepting
me and thank you for being the best mother-in-law a girl could ask for.

To my cousin Shawn, you were gone too soon and are missed dearly. We love you kuzzo! R.I.P. Shawn Boykin and DeAndre Boykin. Save me a spot when I get there. You are now reunited with your brother DeAndre.

Now, if you haven't already, go like my author page LOVELY ANN.

Also, join my reader's group Lovely Ann's Army and Ladies With Killa Swagg is also my group I have with other authors who have come together, and we started the group so come and join us.
Go follow me on twitter https://twitter.com/shortee1982
Instagram: www.instagram.com/shortee3082/,
www.instagram.com/lovelyann66130/
Snapchat: @shortee3082

Finally, we made it to book 4. I hope y'all enjoy these characters because they took me through the most as I was writing this book. They really took me through it, but I finally finished it, so I hope you enjoy them like I did.

Synopsis

They say everything happens for a reason but recent tragic events in Sidney's life have caused her to fall in deep despair and to question whether her and Cameron's love is strong enough to survive.

The results of Sean's evil deeds has formed the bond between the former foes Sidney and Patience. Thanks to the help of her new friend Sidney, Patience is able to turn her life around and start a new relationship with Kareem.

But with Sidney on the verge of losing her sanity and Kareem's emotional distance in the news of Sean's disappearance in which everyone's a suspect, will these 2 couples get there happily ever after or will their love and lives come crumbling down?

Where we left off...

Sidney

Two weeks ago, I found out I was pregnant and now sitting in the doctor's office waiting to be called back to do this paternity test to see if Cameron is this baby's father. I knew Cameron would be the dad no matter what the test said but I still needed to know. As I sat there waiting to be called, Cameron walked in. He couldn't make it on time today because he had practice. My baby and his team finally made it to the playoffs with the help of my bae and I'm very proud of him.

Soon as he walked in, they called my name. I stood up and walked towards where the nurse was then followed her to the back.

"Can you please take off your shoes and step on the scale for me?"

Soon as I looked at the scale, I saw I gained about five pounds. I was happy, but I was also sad. I put my shoes back on and we followed the nurse to a room where she took my vitals there.

"Ok, the doctor will be in shortly, Ms. Smith. Have a good day."

"Thank you and you do the same."

The nurse turned and walked out, leaving us to sit here and in our thoughts. I still couldn't believe Sean was finally gone and can never hurt me again or the fact I was finally pregnant. I felt so amazing right now. I'm gonna love this baby no matter who the father is. If it just so happens to be Sean, so be it. This was still my baby and I couldn't make him or her pay for something they had no control over. There was a knock at the door and the doctor walked in.

"Well, hello again, Sidney. How are we feeling so far?"

"Hey, doc. I'm feeling ok. Just wish this morning sickness would go away."

"Well, you should feel better in about a month or I can give you something for it. Whatever you decide to do. Now, lay back and let's check on this little nugget here." I laid back and lifted my shirt up so the doctor can take a measurement of my belly. "The baby is measuring just fine. Let's see if we can hear the heartbeat today."

I was excited when she said that. It was all becoming so surreal. She squeezed a little bit of gel on the fetal doppler and placed it on my belly. As soon as I heard the heartbeat, tears began to fall down my face.

"Oh my god, that's our baby's heartbeat?" Cameron asked, a little louder than he intended.

"Yes, this is your baby's heartbeat and it's beating nice and healthy."

She removed the fetal doppler and gave me a towel to wipe off my belly. Once I was done, she helped me sit up so could I pull my shirt down and hop off the table.

"Thank you, doctor, for everything."

"You're welcome, Ms. Smith. Now, when you leave out of here, go to the lab and they will draw your blood and the father's as well. You will know the results in three days. I hope everything comes out the way you guys want it to. I will see you guys soon. Make sure you schedule your next appointment before you leave today."

She turned and walked out of the room to tend to her next patient. I grabbed Cameron's hand and we walked to the lab. The closer we got, the more nervous I became. My hands started to sweat, and I slowed down my pace.

"Cameron, please don't leave me if the results are not what we want it to be. I love you and I don't want to lose you. I'm sorry if this isn't your baby. I never wanted this to happen this way."

"I'm not going anywhere so you can hang that shit on up. Like I've been saying since we found out you are pregnant, I am going to be this child's father no matter what. When he or she is born, I want to adopt the baby. Now, let's go in here and get this DNA test done so we can get this shit out the way."

Shit, he didn't have to tell me twice. I checked in and waited for a tech to call me back to get my blood drawn. We were sitting there waiting for about ten minutes before the tech finally came out and called my name.

As I walked toward the tech, she looked like she had an attitude, but I wasn't gonna dwell on it. I was ready to submit this blood and get the fuck out of here, so I just kept it to myself, but Cameron's ass just had to say something with his mean ass.

"Damn, little mama. You don't love your job, do you? Well, you should have gone for something better than a lab tech."

"Excuse you, sir, but you don't know me to say I'm not happy with my job or that I don't love what I do. If you'd like to know, I'm just not having a good day. If you'd please just follow me so we can get this over with, I can head home for the day. I'm sorry if it seems like I have an attitude towards the both of you, but I really don't." We all walked towards the back and went into the room where she had us set up. "Ok, so it looks like they have me drawing blood from you and from the possible father of the child, is that correct?"

"Yes, that is correct, and the possible father is right here. The other is dead so I guess his might be on file with the police if we need it, but these two are the only two possibilities."

5

"There is no explanation needed. I'm not judging you in any way, it happens sometimes. Let's just get this out the way so you guys can be on your way."

I sat in the chair and she walked over with all the things she needed to draw both of our blood. I thought of what the results would be and how they could affect us as a family. I really was starting to fall for Cameron and fast. To some, it may seem soon, but the heart wants what the heart wants; I can't help what my heart wants. We finished up and headed out to the front lobby to schedule my next appointment before we headed out the door.

"Sidney, no matter what you may think, I'm not going anywhere. I'm going to be that baby's father regardless. You will love that baby the same, you hear me?"

"I hear you, baby. How 'bout we go get something to eat?"

"I would but I have a few errands to run. I will call before I'm headed home, babe. Matter fact, how 'bout you meet me at the stadium around seven tonight? I got a surprise for you."

"Cameron, what are you up to now?"

"Don't worry 'bout it but dress up real nice. No, matter fact, I will be sending a car for you at 6:45 so you don't need to drive at all."

I didn't know what he was up to, but I was going to find out. Cameron hopped in his car after he helped me to mine and drove off. I was still sitting there wondering what he was up to when there was a knock on my window, causing me to jump in fright. I turned to see Patience standing outside my door, so I hit the button to roll the window down.

"Hey, girl. What are you doing here?" Patience asked.

"Well, we were just checking up on the baby we're about to have. What are you doing here?" I offered.

"I'm just getting a checkup from being released from the hospital. I didn't know you were pregnant. Congratulations, girl, to both of you," Patience went on.

"Thank you, girl. Means a lot coming from you, especially with how things started with us. I'm proud of you; you have made a big turnaround. But hey, I have to get out of here and get dressed. Cameron has something planned tonight and I don't know what he is up to," I retorted whole heartily.

"Ok, girl, you go ahead. I will talk to you later," Patience responded.

She turned and walked towards the doctor's office and I started my car and drove toward McDonald's. I was craving a Mcflurry and some french fries. Since finding out I was pregnant, everything started hitting at once. I was emotional and now these damn cravings. I had never eaten from McDonald's a day in my life but for some reason, that was what I wanted.

I pulled up to the drive-thru, ordered my food, and was on my way to the house. When I made it home, I got my bag, purse, and my Mcflurry then headed inside. Soon as I walked in the door there were dozens of yellow roses all over the house. I was wondering how the hell Cameron pulled this off in very little time because it only took me about thirty minutes to get here. I picked up my phone and called him but got no answer. He was really up to something now. I sat down on the love seat and ate my fries and ice cream then went to go relax in the tub.

When I walked into the room, there were rose petals all over the floor and bed. More rose petals were on the floor trailing to the bathroom and he had my bath water ready for me. I stripped out of my clothes then climbed into the tub to lay back and relax. I must have fallen asleep because I was awakened by my ringing phone. Looking down, I noticed it was my mother, so I answered it.

"Yes, mother, what can I do for you?"

"Wake your ass up and come open this damn door so I can give you this dress and can be on my way, Chile."

"What dress, mama?"

"The one your man told me to drop off to you. Now get your lazy ass up and come open this door before I beat your ass."

"Mama, how would you whoop my ass if the door ain't open for you to get in?"

I got out the tub, grabbed my towel, and wrapped it around my body, heading for the door.

"Girl, don't worry about it. Just do what the hell I said."

Hanging up the phone, I snatched open the door and she stood there with four shopping bags full of stuff.

"He told me to tell you that you are to wear this tonight and he will see you at seven." With that, my mother got into her car and sped off.

Damn, she didn't even tell me she love me or none of that. After I closed the door and locked it, I went back to the bedroom and placed the bags on the bed. I let the water out the tub and walked over to the shower. I washed my body twice then rinsed off before getting out. Drying off, I walked into the room and began to go through the bags. Cameron had got me a bra and panty set, some shoes, a nice strapless dress, and a little jacket to go with the dress if I get cold or whatever, I guess. I put the bra and panty set on then looked down on my phone to see what time it was. I still had an hour, so I got dressed and went back to sleep.

One hour later...

There was a limo pulling up to the house, so I tried to call Cameron again, but he still wasn't answering. I walked out of the house and locked it up. The driver opened the door and I slid inside. Once he closed the door, he got in and pulled off. It felt like we were driving forever until we finally came to a complete stop. It was a minute before the driver finally decided to get out and open the door for me. When I stepped out the car, my mom and dad were standing there waiting for me with their hands held out.

"Ma, Pop? What's going on? Why are y'all here?"

"Girl, just shut your ol' questioning ass up and go with the flow. You always were a nosey little girl," My mother laughed.

I couldn't believe my ma and pop was here, but I grabbed their hands and walked into the stadium. When we walked inside, Lyfe Jennings was playing.

It feels like something's missing, but I just don't know,
It's like I'm not the same man that I was, no more
And all these crazy places that I usually know,
Are just not as exciting as they were before.
I think about you constantly, it surprises me how I've changed,
My friends are coming down on me, saying a playa never changes the game

We walked further into the stadium and headed out to the field. The closer we got I saw Cameron and his teammates but what surprised me was, Cameron on one knee. His back was towards his teammates so they weren't in no huddle, but they were all dressed up. Walking further, I realized Cameron's family was here along with everybody from my shop. Looking at my mother and father, they had smiles on their faces, so, they knew about this all along. As I got closer, I noticed that he had a ring box in his hand. That's when the waterworks began.

"What your ol' crybaby ass crying for now? The boy ain't even said two words to your ass yet," my Pops said. That man had no filter; he said whatever came to mind no matter where we were.

"Cameron, what are you doing, bae? Why is everybody here?" I asked question after question.

"Just come on over here and I will tell you what's going on, bae," he replied. I stood in front of him and waited for him to continue. "Look, Sidney, I decided this was the best way for this. I wanted everybody in our lives to be present for this day because it means a lot to me. Before I get sidetracked, I want you to know that I love you with all my heart and soul."

"I love you, too, baby. Now, what are you talking about?"

I looked around at everyone here and then I noticed Lucas and his family, and the rest of the crew and I guess their family was here as well. Everyone had their phones out recording this moment. I turned back and looked down at Cameron as he began his big speech.

"I know we ain't been together long, but I love you anyway. I know you are the one for me and I don't want anybody else but you. When I first saw you in the shop and then again at the club where I brought you to VIP, you could have left and never talked to me again after everything went down, but you didn't. You gave me another shot the next day and that spoke volumes in my book. Since that first date, things have changed for the better. You are now pregnant with our baby, praises God for this miracle, and now I wanna know will make me the happiest man and be my wife?"

By this time, I was in a full out ugly cry, trying to wipe my face as I nodded my head.

"Yessss, oh my god, yesss, baby!" I shouted in excitement.

Everyone laughed at me, but I didn't give a damn. I was happy my man proposed to me and we were having a baby. I'm glad I saved all my love for this man right here. He placed the ring on my finger and when I looked down, I saw that it was the ring I always wanted. It was a princess cut diamond frame in 10k white gold. I turned towards my Ma and Pops. My mom was crying, and Pops were smiling real big.

"Now I know you are hungry, so I had dinner catered here for us and everybody else."

I turned to see Gates Barbeque workers walking in with trays of food. He knew I loves me some Gates, so I was cool with that. I sat at the table he had set up on the sideline of the field and began to tear this damn food up.

Two hours later, we were in the limo headed home and I was ready to give my baby a proper thank you. I couldn't contain myself, so I raised the divider. I leaned over and released the monster between Cameron's legs. Getting on my knees, I began to lick the tip of his dick then deep throated him; causing him to moan. I knew I was getting to him because he was pushing my head further down, trying to push his dick to touch my tonsils. I was making it messy just like he liked it. We came to a stop about ten minutes later and I realized we were pulling up to the house.

"Let's take this in the house, Ma."

Shit, he ain't have to tell me twice. I hopped out and went to unlock the door and Cameron was right behind me. He locked the door as I began to strip out my clothes and walk towards the dining room. It didn't take long for him to come out of his clothes.

"You might as well lay your ass spread eagle right here on this table so I can taste this pussy."

I lay on the table like he asked and began to play with my pussy until he smacked my hand away.

"Nah, ma, I got that. You don't need to do that."

Next thing I knew, he dove headfirst and began to go to work on my pussy.

"Awww fuck! I'm cumming already." I released all over his face.

"Damn, girl, that shit right there will drown a nigga."

I laughed at his crazy ass, but my laughter died when I felt his monster enter my pussy. Cameron grabbed my legs and placed them in the crook of his arms, hitting my g-spot.

"Awwww fuck, baby, I'm cumming again."

"Cum all over this dick, girl. Shit, this pussy is so damn wet. I love pregnant pussy."

I was still cumming when he lifted me up and pressed me against the wall, hitting me deeper and deeper while making me reach my climax again.

Cameron, baby, I'm cumminggggg."

"Damn, girl, you cumming again? That's that good shit, huh? Shit, I'm cumming, Ma."

Three strokes later, he was releasing all his seeds in my love box. We slid down the wall and sat there with his dick still inside my pussy. I slowly whined my hips and his eyes rolled to the back of his head. It must have felt good to him because within five minutes he was cumming again and so was I.

"Awwwww fuck, baby, I'm cumming."

"Shit, me too, ma. Me, too. Aggghhhh fuck."

I got off his lap and lay down on the floor to catch my breath. Before I knew it, I dozed off.

The day of the results…

We were sitting around the house waiting for the mail to come so we could find out who the baby's father was. I was getting nervous and anxious about these results.

"Baby, will you stop worrying? I told you I am going to be here for our baby regardless of what they say."

"I know, bae, but I'm just scared this baby might actually be Sean's."

"It doesn't matter 'cause he ain't here to take you through any more bullshit."

I heard everything he was saying but I still worried he wouldn't want to marry me after the results come back. I was actually praying this was Cameron's baby. We sat around the house talking and laughing, trying to get our minds off the results we were waiting on.

Knock, knock!

Cameron got up to open the door and I saw it was the mailman. He snatched the mail from him and slammed the door in his face. He just had to be so rude sometimes. Cameron started going through the mail 'til he found what we had been waiting for.

"Here it is bae. You wanna open it or you want me to open it?"

"I'll open it I guess," I said quietly as I took the letter from him. "Ok, before I open this letter, I just want you to know that I love you more than anything in this world. I hope no matter what the results of this DNA test are we stick this out together and raise this baby."

"Baby girl, I'm here for the long haul so there is no getting rid of me; period. Now, quit stalling and open that damn letter so we can find out."

I slowly opened the letter, but I guess I was taking too long because Cameron snatched it out my hands. He read it then handed it to me. When it came to Baby Smith, there was a 99.99% chance that _____ _____.

Chapter 1

Cameron

*a*s I was sitting there opening the letter from the diagnostic center, I was nervous as hell wondering am I the father or not. I was scared to even read these results. I know I wasn't going anywhere but how will that make me feel knowing that this child ain't mine? I snatched the letter out and read the results and it said: When it comes to Baby Smith, there was a 99.99% chance that Sean is the father. I dropped my head down; I couldn't believe that this was his baby. After all this time, hoping and praying that this was my baby. I still didn't know what was going on. Sidney snatched the paper from me, and she read the results and soon as she read them, she started crying.

"Baby, how is it possible that it is you're not the father, but he is? We had sex first. It just doesn't make sense to me," she cried, holding her head into her hands.

"I don't know babe but either way I'm still going to raise the baby as mine anyway and I'm adopting the baby soon as it gets here since Sean is no longer in the land of living."

I was shocked as fuck. We really thought that this was going to come out as my baby. But I mean, it is what it is. Looking over at Sidney, she was still just standing there with a shocked look on her face. I had to snap her out of it though so we could get to the hospital for her checkup. I walked over to where she was, and I kissed her cheek.

"Babe, look, go get dressed and get your stuff together so we can go. I will be waiting outside for you. Come on; put some pep in your step."

Sidney turned to walk off and I smacked her on her ass. I was happy but also sad that it said I wasn't the father of the baby. I walked out the house and went to start my car, so it could warm up. Shit, this KC weather is funny; one minute it's hot as fuck then it could be raining or cold outside and today, it was kinda chilly. I hate when it's cold outside. I would rather it be spring and summer time. Those were my favorite times of the year. Looking up, I saw Sid coming out of the house, so I climbed out of the car and went to her side to open her door for her to climb in. I ran back around to my side and hopped back in then sped off to the hospital. I turned on the radio and Keyshia Cole *Incapable* was playing.

"It's time to grow up
I embarrass myself enough
'cause I wouldn't leave you ooh
Even my family know the truth yeah, yeah
You've taken me under."

Pulling up to the hospital, we hopped out of the car and went inside. Sidney walked up to the front desk to check in as I went and found our seats. Soon as she was finished, she came and sat next to me.

"Baby, I hope that the baby being Sean's doesn't push you away from me and you stick around for us. We can always try again to have another baby after about 2 years or so."

"I'm not going anywhere. I wish you would stop thinking that I would leave because I'm not. You had no control over what that sick ass nigga did to you. And you damn right; we gonna have another one. Imma keep yo' sexy ass barefoot and pregnant."

Sidney nodded her head and we both sat there in our thoughts. I was wondering how this could happen or even how this was possible since I was the first person to hit that and nut all up in that pussy. So yeah, I was in a state of shock.

"Ms. Smith, you can come on back."

We both stood up and walked towards the nurse that called her name.

13

"That's us", I stated.

"Let's walk over to the scale and I want you to remove your shoes and step on up for me please."

We walked into the room where she weighed Sidney. Soon as she was done getting her weight, she had us follow her to another room where she got her blood pressure and temperature.

"Ok, the doctor will be in here in a second. Here is a blanket. I will ask you to get undressed from the waist down please."

She turned and walked out, and Sidney took her clothes off from the waist down just like the nurse asked. As she was taking her pants off, I got a glimpse of her nice, tight pussy. Oooohhhh and an ass shot, too. I rocked up instantly. Damn that ass is fat, though and her being pregnant had me wanting her in the worst way. That doctor better hurry up so I can hurry home and climb up in the nice juicy pussy.

"Cameron Hill, if you don't take your eyes off of my pussy nigga, you ain't getting any more right now so you might as well hang that up."

"Girl, hush. I can stare at the juicy pussy if I want to and besides, you're gonna give me some soon as we get home. You might wanna hush that talk up; you know you can't resist this monster anyway."

I grabbed my rock-hard dick and her eyes grew big in size like she wasn't expecting me to grab my shit and all. I stood up and walked over to her. I knew the doctor was gonna take a minute anyway. Shit, everybody knows how slow Truman was.

"Ummm, bae? What are you doing? We are not about to be fucking in this hospital."

I got to the bottom of the bed that she was sitting on. I dropped my joggers and freed the one-eyed monster and began to stroke him to life. I lifted the shit she had covering her bottom half of her body. And just looking at this sweet pussy made me want to stop and get a taste, but we didn't have time for that. Her pussy was already wet anyway. I knew she wanted this dick, she was just trying to play that role but I was getting ready to show her all the perks of having all this dick in her life. She pushed my chest soon as I got to her opening, but I rubbed my dick on her clit. It was driving her crazy and I smirked at her; I knew I was getting to her.

"Boy, if you don't quit teasing me imma fuck you up."

I started laughing while backing up and pulled my pants up. She was gonna get this one but soon as we get home, she was hopping on this dick.

14

"Just wait till we get home. You gonna get this meat as soon as we pull up to the crib. So, don't be acting scared when we get there 'cause you know what time it is, gurl."

Sidney just shook her head; she knew I wasn't playing with her ass though. There was a knock at the door and the doctor walked in.

"Hey, mom and dad. How are we doing today? Are we ready to see how the baby is doing?"

Sidney replied, "Well, the DNA results came in today and it said that Sean was the father and not Cameron. We can't wait to see how this little nugget is doing in there."

"Well, let me go get the ultrasound machine and we will take a look to see what's going on in there," the doc explained.

The doctor turned and walked out. We waited for a few seconds for the doctor to return and soon, she knocked once on the door, coming in with what I guessed to be the ultrasound machine.

"Ok, let's take a look at this little peanut and see what we have here."

She pushed the machine to the end of the bed that Sidney was sitting on. "Ok, lay back and let's take a look. I'm going to use this one since you are still early on in your pregnancy. This will be the best way to view the baby."

Sidney laid back and the doctor took out this thing that looked like a dick and slid on a condom like thing onto it.

I interrupted the doctor before she could finish. "Hold up, Doc! Where is that going at?"

She laughed then replied, "I have to do an ultrasound vaginally with her being so early on in her pregnancy."

She continued to go on about her business. But I still didn't want that dildo looking thing up in my girl, but I was ready to see the baby anyway, so, I sat there and let the doctor do her thing.

"Ok, let's see what we have here mom and dad."

She had Sidney guide the dildo looking thing into her vaginal area and I looked at the screen where I saw the baby. Tears started flowing and I was shocked by seeing our little baby on the screen. Next thing you know, I heard the heartbeat and that just melted my heart. I knew I was going to take care of this baby no matter what. He or she is my child now.

"Is that little small pea-like thing the baby right there?" I asked, just to be sure that, that was the baby.

The doctor replied, "Yes, it is, and it looks just fine."

Sidney had tears running down her face and so did I. I just hope that she knew that I wasn't going anywhere. I know she is still gonna think that I was gonna leave but I'm in this for the long haul I already asked this big head ass girl to marry me and I'm going to adopt the baby after it's born.

"So, Doctor, when will we be able to find out what the baby is?"

"Cameron, she will have to be 20 weeks before we will be able to determine the sex of the baby. She has about 11 or 12 more weeks to go. Just be patient and Sidney please, please relax as much as you can. We don't want you to overdo it. With you being high risk, we have to take the necessary precautions. If you get too tired or feel any pain, please have a seat or get in the bed. Please don't hesitate to call; I will see you guys back in 2 weeks."

"Thanks, Doc. I will make sure she takes it easy and stays stress-free."

She pushed the ultrasound machine out the room and she walked out. Sidney got up to put her clothes back on. When she was done, we headed to the front desk to make her next appointment. After we were finished, we headed out to my car and headed home. The ride home was a silent one. We were both in our own thoughts. I was thinking of when I wanted to marry her. I want to be married before the baby gets here so I'm thinking within the next 3 or 4 months. I want to be married but I don't know if she will go for it, but we will see. I might just surprise her with a surprise wedding. Pulling up to the house, I pulled into the garage and as I was getting out the car, my phone rang. I looked down to see it was my coach. I opened the door for Sid where she got out and we walked into the house.

"Babe, I want you to go get ready for me. I have to take this call. It's my coach, it might be important."

"Ok, Daddi." She turned, walked off and I picked up my phone.

"What's up, Coach. What do I owe the pleasure of this call?"

"Well, I have called everybody today because I'm canceling practice. I have a family emergency, but we will resume again tomorrow. We have to be ready for these playoffs."

"No problem, Coach. Thanks for letting me know. I hope all is well with your family. See you tomorrow."

I hung up with and headed to the room with Sidney. She was lying in the bed naked as the good Lord made her and she had her pink rabbit out playing in her pussy. That shit is so sexy to me, I swear it is. Walking over to her, I was stripping out of my clothes. I was ready to taste that sweet pussy of hers. Soon as I walked over, I dragged her to the bottom of the bed and started devouring

16

that pussy. She was trying to run and shit like she was about to get away from this tongue lashing that she has been dying for.

I pulled her back towards me and said, "You better quit running from this shit and take it."

She laid back down and became a big girl for daddy. I had her cumming back to back within 2 minutes. I sat up, placed my dick at her opening, and pushed my way in.

"Ssssssssshhhhh, damn daddi! You so deep already. Owwwww Daddi."

I was hitting with the long strokes just like I know she likes.

"Oh, yea mama. Aint that how you like it? You love when I hit you deep?"

I flipped her over where I entered her then hit rock bottom. As soon as I hit her deep, she was throwing that ass back and throwing it in a circle just how I like it.

"Awww fuck, ma! This shit feels so fucking good. Yea, throw that ass back just like that."

I was talking shit and boosting her up to make her work extra hard for this nut that I know she wanted and needed right now. Sidney hopped up and pushed me down on the bed then climbed on top of me where she started riding me like she ain't never rode me before. After about 5 minutes of her riding me like she was riding a bull, I was cumming in that pussy. Her pussy was so wet I wasn't going to be lasting long tonight. Sidney rolled off of me and lay down beside me breathing heavy. I knew she was out of breath by the work she put in, but I wasn't done with her yet. I pulled her to the edge of the bed and had her legs in my arms spreading them legs wide open so I can dive into that tight wet pussy some more.

"You thought I was done with you baby girl? Nah, I'm just getting started. You bout to take this dick."

I plunged right in and began drilling that pussy just how I know she likes it. Spreading her legs wide open I began tearing that wet ass pussy up. She was cumming all over my dick.

"Awww fuck this pussy is so wet baby. I'm bout to cum."

"Fuck, me too, daddy."

Sidney released all over my dick and I released 2 strokes later. I rolled off her, got out the bed to get a washcloth to wash us both up. When I walked back in the room she was already knocked out. That's what that good dick do to you. I washed her up then went back to wash myself up.

I walked out, crawled in behind Sidney, and soon as my head hit the pillow, I was out like a light.

Chapter 2

Kareem

 was currently sitting in the nursery holding my princess waiting on the nurse to discharge her. She had gained some weight and had been doing so good that she is coming home today. Patience was at the house setting her room up getting it ready for her arrival. I'm still shocked that after the loss of her baby and the fight to get custody of her daughter, she's able to step in and play mama to MY daughter. Even though I would much rather that her mother be here as well. Looking down at my daughter, she was the spitting image of her mother and that is hard even though we didn't have the best relationship before she died. I still had love for her for giving me this beautiful gift. But as I stated before, it's a shame that she won't be here to see her grow up. The doctor walking in broke me out of my thoughts.

"Are you ready to take this little princess home now?"

I nodded my head and put her down in the little bed. He handed me the discharge papers and went over everything that I needed to know. While he was talking to me, I began to get Khalilah dressed so I can put her in the car seat I had just bought her.

"So, I will need you to strap the baby in the car seat correctly before I can let you all leave and also, I need you to sign these discharge papers."

I placed Khalilah in her seat while strapping her in then signed her discharge papers. We headed out of the hospital with a nurse by our side. I was glad to finally be leaving this hospital after being here for a little over a month now. Khalilah made a whole lot of progress over the last few weeks and I was glad that my little princess was doing so well now and can finally go home.

The nurse stood at the entrance and I headed the car seat to her and went so I pulled the car around. Pulling up to the entrance, I hopped out, opened the back door, and grabbed the car seat from the nurse placing it inside my truck. I buckled the car seat in and then thanked the nurse. Back in the driver seat, I drove off and headed to the place that I was now sharing with Patience. Driving down the highway with my music on low, I could hear this song that just came out for the fellas that be messing up with their chicks playing through the speakers:

You tell me you love me
But I ain't been feeling it lately
You say you love keeping me fly but
Can't keep me from looking so crazy
Come in at six in the morning'

Man, whoever messed up with this girl I feel so sorry for him. I would never do Patience like that because I don't want to know how it would feel when she did the same thing as I did to her. I pulled up to the crib in record time. There was a sign on the door saying *Welcome home.* I knew this girl had to be up to something and I was all for it today. I hopped out of the car, went to the back seat to grab my princess out, and then walked to the door. I turned the knob and the house was silent as can be. Walking inside, I shut the door, walked in a little more, then flipped the lights on. Everyone jumped out and they whispered, "*Surprise! Welcome home!*" As I said before, I knew this girl was up to something.

"Thank you all for coming out to see my baby. This is a bittersweet day for me because as you all know Khalilah's mother couldn't be here. She passed away during childbirth."

Everyone clapped their hands and I looked up and Patience was coming my way with an unknown little girl in her arms. This must be her daughter that she has with Rick. He must have finally let her have visitations and I was happy. Patience was doing everything Rick asked her to do; she got her a spot and she is working thanks to Sidney. So, it's safe to say things are starting to look up for her. I just wish I could turn my feelings off about this situation, but I can't. It's hard to have to see her play nice to this man that she used to sleep with just so she can get her daughter back. He acts like it was her fault that she ended up in the hospital behind this man Sean.

"Hey, Kareem. This is my daughter Alyssa. Rick let me have her for a couple days. This is a step in the right direction. Then hopefully, she will be here with us full time before we get married."

I nodded my head as I laid Khalilah in the pink Minnie Mouse bassinet we had set up in the front room. Then, I grabbed the baby out of Patience arms, and she came right to me then laid her head on my shoulder. The baby looked to be about 6 months give or take but it really didn't matter because soon as Patience got full custody, I was going to be helping her raise her. Plus, we were planning our wedding next year, so I was going to be her step daddy anyway. Laughing to myself, I just shook my head because I never saw myself as anyone's stepdaddy but hey, oh well. If we wanted more kids, we could adopt later on down the line. I was just so caught up in my thoughts that I didn't notice that Sidney and Cameron walked up to me until they were tapping me on my shoulder trying to get my attention.

"Aye, yo, my nigga, Kareem. You don't hear us talking to you?" Cameron asked, tapping me on my shoulder repeatedly.

"Aw, my bad, bro. I was spaced off thinking about the future with my family. What did you say though?"

"I was congratulating you on your baby girl and I see Alyssa has taken a liking to you. That's good. She needs somebody like you and I'm glad she has you, dog."

Alyssa looked up when she heard Cameron and she reached for him when she saw him. I knew that Patience said she and Cameron used to be involved but I didn't know how deep it was until Alyssa reached out for Cameron and he grabbed her. She laid her head on his shoulder and started sucking her thumb till she fell asleep. I was shocked because I didn't know if he had ever been around her like that, but I guess so. Looking at everything going on it just all was too much for me. I just wanted to be alone, so I grabbed my baby and headed upstairs. I know I was wrong for just walking off, but I just couldn't help it right now; I needed to be alone. Walking into the baby's room it was a Minnie Mouse set up with her a crib. Patience really did up my baby girl's bedroom. I laid her down in the crib then walked to the room me and Patience shared together. I grabbed some shorts and a tank top then headed to the bathroom to jump in the shower.

I turned it on to the temperature of my liking as I hopped in and began to wash my body with my Axe body wash. As I was washing, I began to think of my baby mother Khalilah and her not being here this was really taking a toll on me. I just wanted to be able to be happy but knowing that she will not be here to help take care and raise our daughter was hard on me for real. Even though I know we created her off of a one-night stand but still, I had love for her and didn't want her to die. If I would have known this would happen, if she went through with this pregnancy, then I wouldn't have made her keep the baby. But I also think she didn't want to get rid of her anyway and she would have fought me on that. Feeling a cold breeze, I knew it was Patience who had walked in the room.

"Babe, I will be out in a minute and be back downstairs so we can entertain our guest."

"Too late, babe. Everybody is gone. After you came up here, everyone left so here I am."

I looked out the shower curtain to see she was stripping out of her clothes. My woman was bad as fuck I swear. Just looking at her naked body my dick rocked up and I was ready to climb up in that pussy. I hope Alyssa was sleep 'cause I was 'bout to climb up in that shit. Patience was bout to call my name. I had a lot of built up aggression and Imma take it out on that pussy.

"Is Alyssa sleep, babe?"

"Yea. I just put her down for a nap. Why, what's up, bae?"

"Cause you bout to get this dick."

Patience climbed in the shower with me and she bent down when she saw my dick standing at attention. She took my pole in her mouth and just started to go to work. She was sucking the soul outta me and I ain't never had any shit like that before.

"Damn, baby. You are sucking that dick. Fuck yea, just like that baby."

I started fucking her mouth and she was taking that shit like a pro. About 2 pumps later I was coating her throat with my nut. Standing her up, I lifted her over my head and began to suck her pussy like my life depended on it. Shit, to me my life did depend on this shit. I love eating her pussy and being up in that wet gussy shit.

"Awww shit daddy, yes, eat this pussy nigga."

Patience was cumming instantly, but I needed to get one more up out of her before I slide her down on this pole. I began to attack her clit as I placed a finger at her entrance as she was riding my face. I knew she was getting ready to cum again and I was waiting for that shit. Next thing I knew she was squirting all in my mouth. I ain't never had a bitch do that but I was all for it today. She released all she had then I lowered her down on my pole and slid up in that tight, wet gussy pussy and began to slam into her. still holding on to her legs I was lifting her up and down as I was working that pussy.

"Aww, shit daddy! You are beating this pussy up. Yesss! Fuck yes, daddy! Just like that!"

"This pussy is so damn wet, baby. Yes! Fuck! I might not last much longer but fuck it, you got a long night ahead of you."

I continued to go to work on that pussy as I felt my nut building with each stroke, I sent to that honeypot. Her pussy was gripping the fuck out of my dick. Patience was gripping my dick so hard that I began to cum all up in her shit. I was coating her walls with my nut.

We both moaned, "Awww, fuck. I'm cumming."

I let her down then turned and grabbed the washcloth to begin to wash us both up as we could get out of the shower because the water was getting cold. Stepping out, I grabbed my towel and Patience grabbed hers. I wrapped my towel around my waist and walked into the room. I grabbed my briefs out my dresser drawer along with my ballers and put them on. Seeing Patience walk out with her towel wrapped around her body did something to me, but I had to put a hold on that right now because Khaliah was crying. I adjusted my dick and walked out of the room while Patience was getting dressed, walking into my baby girl room. Picking Khaliah up, I placed her on the changing table and grabbed a diaper to change her. Khaliah stopped crying after I picked her back up as we walked out and went down to the living room. I grabbed her bag and got a ready-made bottle I had from the hospital and placed the nipple on so I could feed my little princess. As I sat on the couch out the corner of my eyes, I saw Patience coming down the stairs. She was holding Alyssa, so my guess is she didn't take a long nap. Patience came to sit by me, and I kissed her forehead then did the same to Alyssa.

I leaned up and grabbed the remote to turn on the TV, putting it on Netflix to find something to watch. As I was scrolling, I saw that they had a new movie coming out called Nappily Ever After with Sannaa Lathan, but it wasn't available yet so I just selected Til' Death Do Us Part and we sat there with the babies to watch the movie. This was the life that I've always wanted and I'm glad that I finally have but not at the extent of my baby mother. But I was going to work on getting through it. As we were sitting there watching the movie, I was thinking about having to get ready for the funeral Saturday and I had to take my daughter to say goodbye to her mom that she will never get to meet. Just thinking about it really put me in my feelings but I was trying to get it together and enjoy my day with my little family. After I finished feeding the baby and burped her, she went back to sleep, so I laid her in her bassinet and continued to enjoy our time watching this movie. I laid back on the couch and Patience laid back between my legs as Alyssa was laying on her chest. We laid there and enjoyed our time together. Just lying there watching the movie and fell asleep.

Chapter 3

Sidney

S

itting here thinking about these results I couldn't believe that my baby was Sean's and not Cameron's. It broke my heart but there is nothing I could do about it now. I'm not getting rid of my baby; this is something that I have always wanted. Picking up my ringing phone, I saw that it was my shop, so I answered it. I wonder what Erika wanted; I hope that it wasn't anything wrong.

"What's wrong, Erika? You never call me when I'm not in."

"Boss lady, it's a police officer here wanting to talk to you. So, I think you should come in and see what they want."

"Ok, Erika, I am on the way. I will be there in about maybe 20 minutes. Let them know I'm on the way."

"Ok, boss lady. I got you. See you soon."

Hanging up the phone, I knew this was going to happen. I got up and walked up to the room to tell Cameron I will be back in a little while.

"Where you think you going, girl?"

"I have to go to the shop. The police are there and I'm sure it has to do with Sean since he is dead and gone."

"Let me get dressed and I'm going to go with you, babe."

"Ok, babe. I will be waiting on you downstairs."

I turned and walked back downstairs. I was really hoping they didn't come after me for his death. If they found him, I don't know what Lucas and his crew did with his body and I didn't want to know. But I wasn't telling these damn police anything because it wasn't their business. Looking up, I saw Cameron walking down the stairs. I grabbed my phone and the keys, and we headed out the door and on our way to the shop. Cameron opened my door for me, and I got in the driver's seat of the car and put my seatbelt on as Cameron walked around to the other side and he got in and I started the car up and pulled out the driveway and headed to the shop. Hooking my phone up to my radio, I pressed play and *Ocean* by TK Kravitz feat Jacques blared through the speakers.

I'm lying if I said I didn't want it
I can tell by your eyes that you focused (that you focused, yea)
Come and hop on this pony (come and hop on this pony)
Can I dive in your ocean? (Your ocean)
Can I dive in your ocean?
Can I dive in your ocean?

It took me about fifteen minutes to get to the shop. I pulled into my parking spot as Cameron and I got out and walked inside. Everyone looked at me; guess they were happy to see me since I haven't been in since I found out that I was pregnant. I know that I have to come back sooner or later but I had to get some rest first and take it easy. I don't want to lose this baby; this may be my last chance that I have to carry a one.

"Hello everyone. Detectives, please follow me to my office and we can talk back there."

We all walked back to my office and I walked over to my desk and sat behind it as Cameron came and sat next to me on top of the desk.

"You fellas can seat right there."

"Thanks, Sidney. So, we are here because we have received a report from Sean White's wife that he has not been to see their children and we would like to ask have you seen him recently?"

"Well, I haven't seen him since you guys arrested him when he choked me and tried to kill me in front of the officers after he broke into my house and destroyed it."

"Well, if you see him, could you give us a call? Here is my card. Please call us anytime."

They got up and walked towards the door and stopped but turned around again and said, "Mr. Hill, how are you involved with any of this may we ask?"

"Well, officer. This is my fiancée and the mother of my child. I've only met Sean once and that was the day that he tried to choke her in front of her house. Other than that, I don't know him."

"Alright, well, if you two see or talk to Mr. White, please give us a call please."

We both nodded as they turned and walked out the door. I just shook my head while Cameron pulled out his phone and he sent a text that I was guessing was to Lucas. I just couldn't believe Sean's ex-wife was looking for him after all this time. I mean, it's been a few months now that he has been missing and she is just now saying something and going to the police? I just was shocked as fuck, but I was going to check this bitch if she came at me sideways. I know she was the one to send the police my way when she knows I don't fuck with him and ain't fucked with him in 2 years now. Why would I start again?

"Babe, lets head out. I don't want to talk in the shop. Anybody could hear us in here."

We walked out and I let them know that I should be back to work in the next couple of weeks. I can do some hair. Shit, I miss coming into my shop and doing hair anyway. We got to the car and I got in the passenger side this time to let Cameron drive.

"OK, babe. So, I just got done texting Lucas and he said that there is nothing that can trace Sean to us and that his body will never be found. They disposed of his body very well. See, that's why I fucks with Lucas and his crew. They come and they take care of business."

"Ok, Cameron. I just don't want this to come back and bite us in the ass. I want to be around to raise this baby with you."

"We both will be around to raise our little peanut. There is no doubt about that. Now let's head home and get you back in bed."

We drove off towards the house. I was in my own thoughts of hoping this baby will be ok and make it to full term. I was praying for a little girl. I know Cameron probably wanted it to be a boy but shit, long it's healthy I didn't care either way. Pulling up to the house I noticed that Lucas and his brothers were sitting in the driveway. I didn't know they were coming by the house but shit, oh well. I need to go in here and cook cause my ass stayed hungry since I found out I was pregnant. I noticed that their women were with them and I was really starting to wonder what was going on. Cameron got out and came around to open my door and I got out the car while saying what's up to everybody. I headed into the house so I can go cook some fried chicken, mashed potatoes, corn, and

some cornbread. Shit, that's what I was craving right now. I know I
was being anti-social, but my ass was starving right now and that was
the only thing that was on my mind. I heard everyone walk in the house as
I was preparing the food.

"I knew yo ass was in here trying to find some damn food. You need to
have that ass in bed I can cook it for you."

"Boy, please. I'm bout to cook and you can go sit down with yo' friends
and let me handle this. I'm pregnant, not a handicap. Now, get out
my kitchen and let me cook." He began to walk out but I stopped
him. "Babe, are they all staying for dinner, too?"

"Umm, let me ask and see right quick. I will be right back." Cameron
walked out and I heard him yelling. "Aye, y'all niggas wanna stay
for dinner? Bae in there cooking some fried chicken and shit."

"Hell, yea nigga. Fried chicken is my shit. The fuck you thought this
was nigga?"

That must have been the nigga they call Trent. I heard he is petty as fuck
and has no filter. I just shook my head. Cameron came back in the
kitchen like I didn't hear what was said. I just nodded my head
and continued to wash the chicken off and began to prepare the food. As
I was preparing the chicken to put it in the pan to fry it up, I heard
someone walking in the kitchen. I looked up and noticed four
women walking in.

"Hey there, my name is Olivia. I am Lucas' wife, and this here is
Brooklyn, who is Trent's crazy ass wife. Mia is engaged to Mason
and Kaylee is dating Snoop hoe ass."

I laughed and replied, "Well, it's nice to meet you lovely ladies. Would
you ladies like something to drink? I have wine; red or white or water."

"Well, how bout we have a glass of red wine and we can help you cook
if you would like," Kaylee replied.

I reached up to get 4 wine glasses and grabbed the bottle of red wine.
I opened and started pouring them some then handed them each of them
a glass. We all talked a little more as we continued to cook dinner for
the fellas. There was a knock on the door, and I walked out the kitchen to
see the men were no longer in the front room, so I walked to the door
and looked out the peephole and it was Kareem and Patience. I
was wondering what they were doing here. I opened the door and
they walked in when I stepped back to let them in.

"Hey, you two, what are you guys doing here?"

"Cameron called and invited us over. I hope you don't mind," Patience replied.

"That's fine with me. The more the merrier. I'm just in the kitchen cooking with the ladies. You can lay the babies down in one of the spare bedrooms. Kareem, the fellas are all downstairs in Cam's man cave. You go on down there if you would like. It's straight down these stairs."

"Thanks, I will lay this lil' lady down and head on down there."

They both walked upstairs and headed to lay their children down while I headed back to the kitchen to finish up cooking. The food was almost done. We were just waiting on the cornbread and the mashed potatoes.

I was walking around the kitchen grabbing plates and silverware to set the table for us to have dinner as me and the ladies were getting to know each other when Patience walked in the kitchen to ask if I needed any help with anything. I nodded and told her she can grab some cups out the cabinet and bring them to set the table while the other ladies were bringing the food out so we could eat. I walked in the kitchen and checked the cornbread and took it out of the oven and walked it to the table too. I was getting kinda tired, so I grabbed a bottle of water and took a seat at the table and let them know one of them could finish up the potatoes while I sat down and took it easy for a minute. This baby was really kicking my ass. I was about 3 months along now and I was getting excited but nervous at the same time.

"Ok, girl. The food is done now and Imma put it on the table for you And you go get the fellas. You look tired, boo."

"Olivia girl, I am. This baby is kicking my ass and I'm only 3 months along."

"Oh, girl I feel your pain. I'm 6 months along with my second child. Lucas ass got me again. Right before we got married, I found out."

I was laughing but I just noticed that we all were pregnant except for Brooklyn and Patience. I walked down the stairs to where the men were to hear them talking about Sean. I knew it was a reason they came down to Cam's man cave.

"Hey, fellas, the food is done so come on so y'all can eat."

We all walked upstairs together. Soon as I walked in the kitchen, I took a seat and Cameron took one next to me while everyone sat by their significant others.

"Ok, let's all bow our heads and pray over this food,"
Cameron suggested.

"Nigga, when did you become religious?" Trent said. I knew this fool
was going to say something smart but shit, oh well, it is what it is.

"Fool, I've always prayed over my food so just shut up and bow yo'
damn head so we can eat."

"Whatever. Get to it then man. This food looks hella fire right now."
Everyone bowed their heads and Cameron began to pray over the food.

"Heavenly Father, we ask that you bless those that prepared this food and
bless this food. I ask that you touch those that need to be healed Lord in your
name we pray, Amen."

"Amen," we all said in unison.

It was quiet as we all began to make our plates. Shit, I was hungry as fuck.
There was no talking as we all sat and ate our food. It must have been that good.
I was so focused on my food that I wasn't hearing anything anybody was saying
even if they were talking. This baby had me eating every damn thing.

Cameron began to speak finally. "Ok, let's start this little meeting off so we
can get y'all outta here so y'all can get back to your families."

"Umm, Cam babe? What are you talking about meeting? I didn't know you
were having a meeting here tonight?"

"Well, we have to discuss this Sean situation since the police showed up at
your shop today and I found out they stopped by your old house and questioned
Patience and Kareem. So, we all need to have this meeting."

Lucas then spoke up. "So, you all need to be on the same page so that there is
no mix up if they come back and question you again. My crew cannot go down
for this even though it was to protect all of you guys from that bitch ass nigga
that likes to touch things that don't belong to him."

He sounded angry but shit, I didn't ask any fucking body to get involved and
to kill the nigga. He could have been in jail, I don't give a fuck. But Imma sit
here and listen to what the fuck they got to say for now.

"Now me personally, I would have just done that off GP cuzz. I don't believe
in a man raping a woman to get what he wants and to constantly stalk this
woman? Fuck all dat! He deserved to die, and I gives no fucks about it," Trent
laughed.

This nigga was really laughing like the shit he said was fucking funny, but I
didn't because somebody being dead wasn't a joke but whatever. It is what it is.
Sitting here looking around the table, I saw people was actually laughing at this
stupid nigga.

"Ok, look. I'm not changing my story. Patience, when they came by the house, what did you tell them, girl?"

"I told them that I hadn't seen him since he beat my ass and made me lose the baby and now, I can't have any more kids!!!"

She was now crying, and I felt bad that I even had to bring her into this as it is. She didn't deserve this at all even though in the beginning, things started off bad between us but hey, she is a changed woman and I'm all here for that. Shit, if I can have a baby for her, I would do that shit because everyone deserves to be happy and have as many kids as they want to. I was going to talk to her about it and see if it's still a possibility that she has her ovaries then maybe I can carry a baby for them. When they are ready, they can let me know. Who knows, it could be a year or maybe two when they will be ready. I know she is still healing from the loss that she had.

"Look, Patience, I have been where you are. He beat me so bad that I lost my baby as well so trust me, I know how you are feeling."

Brooklyn spoke, "Listen, Patience is it?" Patience nodded her head. "I've also been where you are except mine was not how neither one of you have lost your babies. I've been pregnant so many times and each time I get pregnant, I end up losing the baby. This last time I was seven months, I went into early labor and delivered a lil' boy. Man, he was the spitting image of his father. He had so many health issues such as his lungs were underdeveloped, he was placed on oxygen, he had bleeding on the brain and many other issues. He didn't make past 3 days. His name was Trent Jr and I have pictures to show you guys but not right now, y'all will get me to start crying."

"Man, look. We getting off topic, but everybody needs to stick to their story so none of us have to go down for this fuck nigga's murder," Lucas spoke with finality. Everybody nodded their heads and agreed. "Now, I think that was it. I need to go smoke a blunt so I'm stepping outside. Come on fellas. Leave these ladies to whatever they need to do, and we can go smoke."

Cameron and all the other fellas got up and headed out back by the pool. And I had to run and go to the bathroom. My stomach was starting to bother me. Running as fast I can, I never said anything to the ladies as I just got up and ran. But I could hear them behind me. As I got to the bathroom, I couldn't hold it in anymore and before I made it to the toilet, I began to vomit everywhere. Omg, I just can't catch a break with this throwing up mess. I can't wait till I'm completely out of the first trimester because this throwing up shit is for the birds.

"Oh my God, are you ok honey? Olivia asked.

"Yea, I'm ok. This baby is just kicking my ass. I got another month till this is all over and I'm past this stage. I can't wait."

I grabbed a washcloth and began to wet and wash my mouth. Then, grabbing my toothbrush, I brushed my teeth then rinse my mouth out. After finishing everything, I was ok to head back down to the kitchen to start loading the dishwasher, so I can wash these dishes then lay down and watch a movie. I'm in the mood to watch my all-time favorite *Set it Off* with Queen Latifah and Jada Pickett. When I walked back downstairs, the fellas were all coming into the house. I walked over to the sectional couch to sit down and to put a movie in so I could relax.

"Hey, babe. Why your face all red? You been throwing up again?"

"Yea, I did, babe. I'm really not feeling too hot right now so Imma lay here and watch a movie for a little while till I fall asleep maybe."

"Ok well, I'm getting ready to head to practice. If you need anything, don't hesitate to call me and I do mean anything."

"Ok, Cam I will. Call me when you on your way home tonight."

He got up and kissed my head while everyone walked out behind him. I waved to everyone as they walked out. I got up and went to put the movie in the DVD player and walked back over and lay back down on the couch. I was maybe laying there for about a good ten to fifteen minutes before I finally drifted off to sleep. I didn't even clean the kitchen before I lay down, but I will do that when I wake back up.

Chapter 4

Patience

We were walking to the car getting ready to get in when Cameron came over to us. "Hey, I need a favor from you guys please?"

"What's the favor Cam?"

"I need you, Patience, and Kareem to sit with Sidney tomorrow while I handle some business regarding our wedding. She doesn't know this yet, but I've done already purchased her dress and I'm actually going to go look at some venues and hire a pastor for the wedding tomorrow and I need you guys to keep her busy if you have to bring the babies do that shit then but I want to surprise her with the wedding of her dreams. So, she doesn't have to do any work and it will be all done in time. I'm hoping she will say yes to marrying me next Saturday."

"Aw, dawg, you know we got you. I can't wait till we can get married but we going to wait a while, so we can get to know each other a little more."

"Thanks, Kareem, I will get up with y'all tomorrow. Be here by 9am though."

He turned, walked off and jumped in his ride. I put Alyssa in as Kareem put Khaliah in their car seats and strapped them in. We got in the car then headed towards our house. I was so deep in my thoughts I didn't even notice that we were home. It didn't even take us long. I got out of the car still thinking about everything that went down this year. I tried to pin not 1 but 2 babies on Cameron and it ended up backfiring on me. We were no longer sleeping together. I've gotten beaten and almost lost my life behind everything then lost my baby in the process. Now I can't have any more kids at all. Kareem proposed to me and we haven't even been together that long. Rick having custody of Alyssa and me trying to get her back, things were hard but I'm going to get through this and I'm going to get custody of my baby. The shop will be opening soon; I hope right now I just get to visit with her when he allows me to. So far, I've had her for three days. Maybe he was finally coming around now that he sees me trying.

"Patience, you didn't hear me talking to you?"

"Naw, baby. What did you say?"

"I asked you if you can give Khaliah a bath and I will watch Alyssa 'til you are done. I'm still scared to give her a bath right now."

"Yea, babe. I got you. Here, take Alyssa and put on Paw Patrol for her. She should be good to go."

I grabbed Khaliah from him and went to lay her in the crib then got her bathtub and turned the water. I let it run for a second before I checked the water to see if it was just right; not to hot and not too cold. I went into the room and grabbed a diaper, her pajamas, and lotion then sat it all up on her changing table. Then, I grabbed her and got her undressed. I got her towel and baby wash and walked into the bathroom and began to wash her up. She started crying and I was talked to her to get her to calm down. But that wasn't working so I started singing one of my favorite gospel songs; Yolanda Adams, *"Open my heart."* Soon as I started singing, Khaliah stopped crying, so I began to finish up giving her, her bath so we can get her ready for bed. Picking her up, I wrapped her towel around her then walked towards her room to lay her down on her changing table and began to get her dressed. After I was finished, I head back downstairs to go lay her in her bassinet and make her a bottle, so her dad can feed her before she went to bed. Handing it to Kareem he picked up Khaliah and I grabbed Alyssa big butt, so I can go give her a bath as well. I walked in her room which I had decorated in Paw Patrol; her favorite right along with Mickey Mouse Club House and Bubble Guppies, but she liked Paw Patrol more than the others, so this is how we did her room. Sitting her in her playpen, I went to get everything I needed. After getting her pajamas, a diaper, and lotion, I laid them on her changing table and walked in the bathroom and turned the water on the right temperature. Doing that, I walked back to grab Alyssa where I undressed her then put her in the bathtub so she could play with her toys for a little while before I bathe her. I pulled out my phone to see I had a text message from Kareem like he ain't right downstairs.

Kareem: *Hey, I just want to thank you for everything. I know that I don't say it enough, but you stepped up as a mother role for my princess and I can't thank you enough. I love you so much more for what you have done for us.*

Me: *Babe, its NP. That's what I'm here for and I wouldn't have it any other way. I'm gonna always have y'all back no matter what. Lol. I love you, too, now let me finish giving this little girl her bath why she over here splashing water at me and shit.*

Kareem: **kissing emoji**

This boy was something else I swear. I got up and began to wash my baby girl up, so I can get her ready for bed next. As I finished my phone rang. I stood up to see who it was, and it was her father Rick. I wonder what he wanted. I hope he wasn't trying to come and get her because I am not ready to let her go just yet. I yelled for Kareem to come sit with Alyssa while I see what he wants.

"Kareem babe? Can you please come sit with Alyssa because her father is calling. I need to take this."

"Here I come, babe."

Picking up my phone, I sighed before answering. "Hello, Rick. What's up?"

"Look, I can't keep Alyssa anymore. My wife doesn't want her around. She is already mad that I went and had another baby on her. So, I will go ahead and draw up some papers and I will sign over all my rights. I will pay you child support just because I wanna make sure she is taking care of. I know that this may come as a shock to you considering how hard I was on you about getting your shit together, but I can't lose my wife over this."

"Look, I don't even care long as I can keep my baby. I knew it was a reason why you let me keep her this long. Just draw up the paperwork and we can sign this shit and get this over with. I'm just happy I get more time with my daughter now."

"Alright, I will call you in a couple days when my lawyer has the papers drawn up. Then we can meet up so we can sign them. I will holla at you later on. Bye Patience and I'm proud you got your shit together."

The next thing I know before I could respond, he hung up. I couldn't really believe Rick was turning his back on his daughter for his punk ass wife but fuck both of them. I don't give a fuck. If it was that simple for him to turn his back on his daughter, then he wasn't the man that I thought he was. I got up and walked back towards the bathroom to where Kareem and Alyssa were laughing as she was splashing water at him. She loved to splash people while she was in the tub. I walked inside and Kareem noticed my face because as I stated before, I was pissed about how that conversation went with Rick.

"Umm, Patience, what's wrong? You look pissed."

"That's because I am. This fuck nigga called me to tell me that his wife doesn't want my daughter over there, so he is signing over his rights and is having paperwork drawn up. But he also said he will pay child support so he can make sure she good. Just by him saying all that shit pissed me off. Man, I never thought in a million years that Rick would even do our daughter like that. But on a good note, she has you and that's all that really matters right now but it would have been nice for her own daddy to be there and help raise her."

"Look, babe, we are both gonna help raise each other's kids. Fuck that old ass nigga. He wanna be a no-good ass baby daddy and do what his wife says and not be there for his kid then fuck both them bitches. She will grow up to hate that nigga in the long run but hey, let's not talk about this situation anymore until after these kids go to sleep."

I walked over to grab my baby and wrapped her towel around her little body. I walked back into her room and laid her down on her changing table to begin to get her dressed and lotion down her body. Soon as I finished, I picked Alyssa up and we walked down the stairs then headed back to the living room to sit her down on the couch next to Kareem while I went to make her a bottle of warm milk with rice cereal added to it. She loves rice cereal added to her formula at night; it helps her to sleep through the night and she gets full faster. Walking to the kitchen, I grabbed her bottle, prepared her milk, and then placed it in the microwave for 20 seconds. Then, I headed back to the living room and handed her bottle to her where she laid down and began to kick her feet while watching the TV until she finally fell asleep. I left her alone and just sat there in my own thoughts. I was sitting here thinking; why Rick would just not want to be in this little girl's life? Like, she makes everything better when you are feeling sad. That's just not right at all; she needs her father, but I know she will end up hating him when she gets older, but he brought that all on himself. I looked over and Kareem was picking Alyssa up and taking her to her room. I picked up Khaliah and took her to her room while grabbing the baby monitor then headed to my room where I grabbed me something to put on for bed. Then I headed to the bathroom to take me a shower. As I was standing under the water, I felt a cold breeze and looked up to see Kareem walking into the bathroom stripping out of his clothes to get in the shower with me.

"Kareem, what do you think you are doing?"

"Just what it looks like. 'Bout to take a shower with my wife and then 'bout to dig deep in that pussy."

He began to laugh, and I couldn't do shit but laugh. This nigga stay trying to be in my guts like it's just the thing to do right now. But hey, he is putting it down for damn sure. He began to wash my back and the rest of my body while I grabbed his towel to lather his soap on the towel and began to wash him up. After rinsing off our bodies, he dipped down and began to suck the soul outta my pussy. It was feeling so damn good I was cumming instantly.

"Awwww, fuck baby! I'm cumming already."

"Let that shit go, Ma."

Soon as I let go, Kareem lifted up while picking me up, positioned me over his head, and ate my pussy from the air. Oh my God; that shit was everything. I was cumming again in no time.

"Yea, Ma. I feel you squirting, and shit come on and give me that shit."

"Aghhhh fuck baby. I'm cumming again."

Kareem let me down after I released all in his mouth and sat me right on his long thick pole. He was slamming me up and down on his dick and I was loving every bit of it. My pussy muscles were clenching around his dick and he was moaning all loud and I knew he wasn't going to last much longer. Whenever he got up in this pussy he never does, 3 strokes later, Kareem was releasing all up in my honeypot, coating my walls.

"Got damn this pussy be turning me into a minute man but I ain't done with your ass yet. So, you might as well get ready for a long night."

I knew what he was saying was true; he was bout to make me cum over and over all night and it was just what I needed after everything that happened with Rick today. We washed our bodies again then got out the shower, grabbed our towels while drying off, then went right to the bedroom. Soon as I laid down in the bed Kareem dove head first in my honey pot and was eating this pussy like it was going out of style. He made me cum a good 3 times before he lifted up and began to trail kissed up towards my neck. Soon as he was at my opening, I felt him knocking on my entrance, going in and slow stroking my middle. It was feeling so damn good I was cumming in no time. I don't know what he was doing to my body, but I was cumming back to back.

"Damn, babe, what are you doing to me?"

"Shit, making dat pussy cum back to back and wear that ass out 'til you pass out, Ma."

Kareem was beating my pussy up out the box. I couldn't even hold that shit in even if I wanted to. Next thing I know, this nigga was picking me up and he was doing The Melvin; that African nigga squat as Ving Rhames said in the movie Baby Boy. I don't know what it is about that position but we both were cumming in no time. Kareem stood up to let me down and I walked into the bathroom with him behind me where I began to wash up after that beating, he put on my pussy. Shit, yo, girl is tired now and I know I'm going to crash soon as my head hit the pillow. After washing up, I walked out the bathroom, grabbed my t-shirt and panties, put them on, and then laid in the bed. I fell asleep before Kareem even came out of the bathroom.

Chapter 5

Rick

I

    Met Patience about 3 years ago and she was everything to me. I told her when I first met her that I was married and there will never be anything more to me and her but sex. She was ok with that. She was stripping in this club called Shady lady and I loved her moves. My wife just wasn't doing it for me anymore; she started slacking on her job. She wasn't fucking or sucking me like she used to, so it was time for me to find somebody to handle that for me.

Fuck, I'm rude as fuck. My name is Rick and I was Patience Sugar daddy until she got with this new nigga Kareem. I don't know where she met this nigga but she didn't have him before she ended up in the hospital after some nigga beat her fucking ass. She left my daughter with this low life Dolla and I wasn't having it, so I put him out of my condo I had got for her and I took my daughter. Now, I'm paying for it because my wife of 26 years found out that I was having an affair and had another baby. She told me I needed to get rid of the baby or she was gone. I couldn't lose her sad to say but she is my life and I still needed her money. Little did she know, I was taking her from everything that she had. Yea, I was Patience sugar daddy, but I was using my wife's money to make things happen for Patience. See, my wife was a trust fund baby.

She inherited everything from her father who had passed away some
 years ago.
Now here we are today. I just hung up the phone with my baby mama and
I had just told her that I would be signing over all my rights to our
daughter to her and I really felt bad but what can I do? I can't lose my
wife right now. I know Patience was mad about what I said but I was
still gonna take care of her financially because that is my daughter and I
just can't be there for her right now. As I was sitting here in my thoughts,
I heard my wife's nagging voice.

"Actually, no I didn't. What are you bitching for now? I did what you
asked so what more could you possibly want?"
"You know what? Fuck it! I'm going to bed. I will see you if you come."
She walked off and I was glad she had finally walked away from me and
left me the hell alone. My phone went off and it was a text from my lawyer.
 I pulled it out and read the message.
Ryan: *Hey, the paperwork is drawn up. I will be by there in about 10 to*
 15 minutes to drop it off. When u get it signed, I will take it to
the courthouse and file it.
Me: *Ok. See you soon. Thanks again.*
I put my phone up and again, my wife was standing in front of me
mugging me like I did something to her. I just shook my head, got up
from the couch, and went to the bedroom I was sleeping in. Yea, you
read that right; we sleep in separate rooms. We haven't slept together
 in about seven years and I'm a man that has needs that need to be
met. Walking into my room I went to my walk-in closet and grabbed me
 an outfit to put on then laid it across the bed. I walked back over to my
door and locked it because I didn't trust this bitch as far as I could throw
her. After locking my bedroom door, I walked to the bathroom that was
 in my room and let the water run to the temperature of my liking. I
pulled my phone out and sent Patience a text to tell her where to meet
me and when.
Me: *Meet me at the cheesecake factory in 20 minutes so we can sign*
 these papers. Bring the baby with you so I can see her one last time,
 please.
I wanted for what felt like 10 minutes, but it was only like 5
really.
Patience: *Fine and I'm bringing my fiancée with me, too.*

Me: *That's fine with me. See you soon.*
Hooking my phone up to my Bluetooth speakers, I went to my music to
play some music. The perfect song came on;
Can we get a room
And we ain't gotta tell nobody
It's just me and it's just you
And what we do in here is private
Cut your phone off
Make sure the door is locked
Listening to this song reminded me that I couldn't have Patience but oh
well. I got to get over that right? Right. I jumped in the shower and
grabbed my dove body wash for men and washed my body right quick
then jumped out and wrapped my towel around the lower half of my body.
I walked into my room and began to get dressed so I could head out
to Cheesecake Factory which is only 5 to 10 minutes away from my
house. As soon as I finished getting dressed, I grabbed my phone out
the bathroom and walked out while snatching my keys off my dresser.
I headed out my room and walked right past my wife then out the door.
Soon as I walked out, Ryan was pulling up, so I walked over to his car
and got in as he handed me the paperwork. I got right back out; it
was nothing that needed to be said anyway. I looked up and Michelle,
my wife, was standing at the door watching me. I just waved, got in my
car and drove to the Cheesecake Factory. As soon as I pulled up, I
noticed that Patience, her man, and the kids were walking in. I parked my
car and headed inside. I saw them sitting at a booth and walked over to them
where I had a seat.
"Hey, you two. Nice to meet you. Is it Kareem?"
"You know what my name is but we not gonna get into all that. Let's just
get this over with cause I really don't wanna be around you like that."
I just shook my head. "Ok, here is the paperwork. Go ahead and sign
it and I will leave it to you. Dinner is on me today."
I passed over the paperwork to Patience and she looked it over
then signed where she needed to then passed it back to me so I could sign.
I held my arms out for my little girl and she came right to me. I nuzzled
my nose in the crook of her neck and just whispered in her ear that I
was going to miss her and that I love her. This was really hard on me
though. I looked up and my wife was standing over me looking at me as
I held my baby.

"Oh, so this is why you rushed out of the house to come see this hoe and this bastard child of yours?"

"Look, bitch. I don't know who you are but I'm not a hoe and my baby is not a bastard child. You need to move around. But since you are here, have a seat and let me explain something to your miserable ass," Patience said. Michelle gave her this nasty ass look then sat next to me. "Ok, let me tell you something. I've never been a hoe and my child is not a bastard for one. And two, how can you live with yourself knowing that you asked this man to choose between you and this beautiful little girl? I don't know if y'all have kids or not but you both will miss out on everything involving her and that will be on you and only you. But never in your miserable life will you come for me calling me a hoe. You the one not giving it to your husband. Shit, it's been 7 years since y'all have had any type of sexual chemistry and that is why he came to me for it for so long. Now I'm not interested in having dinner anymore. I lost my appetite but let me leave you with this. You both will take care of all her needs financially and there are no questions asked. Y'all will also pay for her childcare because I will be starting to go to work soon. And since you signed over your rights to Alyssa for this miserable bitch, that's the least you can do. But I will say this, when you want to be in her life, just call me. Hopefully she remembers you. Now, give me my baby and we will be on our way."

I handed Patience the baby and they all got up to leave and so did I. I'm not in the mood to be around this woman right now. She tried to grab my hand but I snatched away from her and walked out. I caught up to Patience and Kareem and stopped and apologized to them for the way that Michelle acted. I told her I will let her know when everything is a go and I will pay for everything that she has requested. Patience nodded her head and walked away. I walked off and hopped into my ride. I was going to get me a hotel because I didn't feel like being around Michelle right now anyway. I was going to be staying at the Best Western tonight. It took me about 20 minutes to get there. I got out, checked in, then walked right to my room. As soon as I got in my room, I turned the TV on and got undressed where I laid in the bed. Soon as I was on my way to sleep my damn phone was ringing off the hook. Picking it up, I saw it was Michelle, so I declined her call and laid back down. No sooner than I was relaxed my phone was ringing again but I declined her call yet again. I turned my phone off and got comfortable but soon as my head hit the pillow, I was out like a light.

Chapter 6

Cameron

Waking up to the smell of bacon, I rose up outta bed and walked into the bathroom to take care of my hygiene. As soon as I was done, I went to my dresser to grab some briefs, some basketball shorts, and a white tee and walked out of the room. Walking into the kitchen, I saw Patience and Sidney chopping it up. I was happy that Patience did a huge turn around after she loss her baby. It's sad that it took that for her to change her life. But now, she and Sidney are close and that is a good thing.

"Girl, I'm telling you, I let both of their ass have it. She called my child a bastard and made him sign over his rights. So, I told both they ass they were paying child support and for her childcare."

"Girl, you are better than me. I would have beat her ass. Don't ever in your miserable life come for me or my child. The fuck is wrong with these bitches these days."

I just walked into the kitchen and kissed Sidney on her cheek after I said what's up to Patience. I went to the living room to watch ESPN. I walked in to see Kareem was in there already watching and the girls were sleep on the couch by him. So, I sat on the couch opposite from him and said what's up and began to watch the coverage they were having on my team. We had lost our last game of the regular season, but we made it to the playoffs. We really thought we had this in the bag, but we ended losing against Pittsburgh.

"Aye, man, thanks for sitting here with Sidney when I go handle this business. I can't just leave her here by herself."

"We got you, don't trip. Now we gonna eat this food they in there cooking and then you gonna get out of here while I keep them entertained. But look, we had one hell of a night last night. We went to meet up with Rick and his wife popped up and started talking shit and then called the baby a bastard child. But check it, Rick signed over all his rights and is still gonna pay her and pay for everything else concerning the baby."

"Damn, bro. That's fucked up. Why is he signing over his rights though?"

"His wife made him is my guess."

"Damn, man."

I always thought Rick would step up when I found out it was his baby, but damn never in a million years did I think that he would sign over his rights to this precious little girl sitting right here. That's fucked up bro, real shit. That man gets no respect from me after this shit. Money will never replace your absence. I don't care how much money you got or that you give the mother. In my eyes, that is wrong as fuck and there will be no coming back from that. As I was sitting here in my own thoughts the ladies came out to let us know breakfast was ready. I got up and went to the dining room to sit at the table while everyone else walked in. Sidney set my plate in front of me and Patience did the same for Kareem and Alyssa. Little mama looked like she was getting ready to throw down on her food.

"Little girl, you better not touch that food yet."

Alyssa gave her mother a look like, "But mom! I'm hungry," and was getting ready to start eating anyway till her mom came and stood over her waiting on her to try her. She knew what she was doing, and she was smart as fuck. I bowed my head and said my prayer over my meal while the ladies got their food and sat in there spots next to us and they began to dig in.

"Patience, I'm sorry that Rick turned out to be a deadbeat but check it, we would love to help you guys with anything y'all need help with, with Alyssa or with Kareem's daughter as well. We are here for both you no doubt."

"You know y'all don't have to do this right? We will be perfectly fine. But as for Rick's bitch ass, fuck him. I don't even care anymore cause really, Alyssa will hate him when she gets older for how he just threw her to the side for that bitch. He thinks money will replace the absence of him not being there, but it won't."

"Look, boo, we will help y'all. We are all friends now so what was done in the past is behind us. Let's all raise these kids and forget about everything else. Now eat so Cameron can get out of here. He has practice in an hour."

I guess Sidney has spoken. For the rest of our breakfast, we all sat and ate in silence. After we all finished, the ladies went to clean the kitchen while I picked up Alyssa and she laid her head on my shoulder and instantly she fell asleep. I walked her up to one of the spare rooms and laid her in the middle of the bed. I walked out of the room to let them know that she was sleep and in the guest room. I walked in the kitchen and kissed Sidney on the cheek and let her know I was headed out and will see her later. I know, I know what y'all thinking; it's too early for us to get married but I want her to have my last name before the baby gets here. So today is the day. I already have her mom getting her dress for her. I found the picture of the dress she wants, and I gave it to her mom, and she is going to get the dress while I'm doing everything else. I grabbed my keys and phone then headed out of the house. I jumped in my car and Meek Mills blasted through my radio.

Look feel the vibe, it's contagious
Look in your eyes, shit is dangerous
Grateful I had all the patience
I know you going through some changes
You taking pictures, know your angles
Ooh, no we ain't perfect, but we damn close

Ooh, you give me something I can't pay for
I pulled up to the Overland Park convention center and walked inside to go pay the people and have them decorate it just what we wanted. As we walked around the convention center, it looked dope like the perfect set up for a wedding. Man, y'all would have to see this place for yourselves to even believe how nice it was on the inside. I know after they get it set up for tonight that it will be just like I pictured it. I paid them and told them what I wanted. I then walked back out to my car to go handle everything else for tonight and then head to practice. I dialed my mom's number to see if she will be ready for tonight. The phone rang 3 times before she picked it up.

"Community dick, what you calling me for? Damn, how you know mama ain't tryna get her groove back?"

"Ma, you doing too much man. You know I'm not giving the community dick. I'm only with one person and that's why I called you. I need you at Overland Park convention center at 8 pm tonight for my wedding and don't be tryna go all off on me cuz I called you at the last minute. Just get that there. Love you, Ma."

Hanging up before she could respond was a good move to tell you the truth cause if I would have let her get another word in, she would have been cussing me out for real. I told y'all moms don't play that shit but let's get on and get back to get this wedding situated so I can get to practice. Jumping back into my car, I headed to the bakery to get the cake, so I could drop it off at my ol' lady house. As I was pulling up to the bakery, my phone went off letting know I had a text come through.

Wifey: *Hey, babe. When you head home, can you stop and get me a Mcflurry and some fries, please?*

Me: *Can you ask Kareem cause I don't know when the coach is going to let us out of practice today since we are preparing for the next playoff game next week. We have to be ready for Atlanta.*

Wifey: *Ok well, have a good practice babe and we love you. See you when you get home.*

Me: *Love you, too, Ma.*

I put my phone in my pocket then got out of the car and headed into the bakery. As I walked in, I saw this chick I used to date back in high school. Her name is Micha Coves. I haven't seen her since freshman year. She must be doing well since she was working in the bakery.

"How can I help you? Are you ordering or picking up today?"

"I'm picking up."

Micha looked up finally and she noticed who I was. "Cameron Hill? Is that you? Oh my god! We haven't seen each other since high school."

"Yea, I know Micha. How you been?"

"Oh, I've been good. Married now with own my own shop. How bout yourself?"

"I'm getting married today and we have a baby on the way. So, yea that's why I'm here I need to pick up our cake."

"Ok. Let me go back here and get it."

I nodded and she turned and went to the back to get the cake. I got it decorated in lavender and like a light blue and then on top of it was the bride dragging the groom. I thought Sidney will get a laugh out of that. Micha came walking back out with the cake and I paid for it and walked it to my car. It was just what I had envisioned. Now for the gender reveal, I just might come here for the cake. I already have the perfect idea for it anyway. I jumped in the car and headed to my mom's crib. It took me about 15 minutes to pull up and I hopped out, grabbed the cake and walked into the house.

"Ma, where you at?"

"Boy, you better quit yelling in my damn house. I'm here in the kitchen. What the hell yo' community dick ass wants anyway?"

"Ma, how many times I got to tell you I've settled down and I'm getting married today?"

"Shit, that doesn't mean nothing. You still just like yo' no good ass daddy spreading yo' wild oats around Kansas City."

I couldn't do anything but laugh at her cause she was always going in on my sperm donor. I don't even know him for real. He got my mom pregnant with me and dipped on her when she told him she but that's another story for another time.

Shaking my head, I said, "Mom, here is the cake. Take it to the convention center when you head over there. I got to get to practice. I will see you later."

I kissed her cheek then turned and walked out. I jumped back in my car and headed to practice. Arriving in no time, I went inside and began to change then headed to the field. I didn't need coach to give me a penalty for being late. Walking on the field, everyone began to cheer me on. Shit, a nigga was the star quarterback, and everyone loved what I could do for the team.

Two hours later…

I was walking out of practice towards my car heading out to my mom's house to go get ready. Before I pulled off, my phone went off. Looking down, it was a text from Sidney.

Wifey: *Ummm, bae. There are these ladies here saying that you sent them to do my hair and makeup and my nails. What is going on?"*

Me: **wink wink emoji** *Well babe, it's a surprise. If I tell you what it is, I'd have to kill ya. Now and we both know I can't go without you, right?*

Wifey: *lol You think you funny, I see. But whatever. I will go with it for now.*

I placed my phone in the cup holder and hooked it up to the car radio. Soon as I turned my music on, Kendrick Lamar blasted through my radio.

Give me a run for my money
There is nobody, no one to outrun me
(Another world premier!)
So, give me a run for my money
Sipping bubbly, feeling lovely, living lovely
Just love me
I wanna be you, ayy, I wanna be with

Lovely Ann

Sidney loves this song. She always playing this damn song all over the house. It was now time to go get ready for this wedding. Hopefully, it will work in my favor and she goes for it. Pulling up to Ma Duke's house, I jumped out and went inside to get ready. I didn't see my mom, so I began to walk around the house. As soon as I got to her room, I heard some moaning. I just shook my head until I heard that very familiar voice. It was my father. I just knew she didn't have this bitch ass nigga in here with her. Shit, after what he did to her when she had my little sister, I don't see why she would give the nigga the time or day. This nigga swore up and down that my sister wasn't his child only because he didn't want his wife to find out that he was cheating on her.

See, my mom and pops was in a relationship way before he got married. Then my mom's found out he was cheating but when he got engaged to the chick, she left his ass. Two months later, she found out she was pregnant with me and he still didn't come back around. He wasn't there for me growing up or nothing. Ten years later, they got back together and then she ended up pregnant again and he denied my sister when the wife found out. I kicked open her bedroom door and they both jumped up pulling the covers over their bodies to try to hide.

"Son, what the fuck is your community dick ass doing in my damn room?"

"Ma, what the fuck you doing in here with this fuck nigga after the way he left you when you were pregnant with little sis? I just can't believe you, Ma. And you." I turned towards my pops. "You are a whole ass married man. Why the fuck is you even here like you ain't got a whole ass wife at home?"

"Look, son, don't worry about what me and your mom is doing. Just get the fuck out of here."

See, this nigga had me fucked up. There is no way in hell I would ever respect this nigga or even be ok with him fucking with my mom's again after all he has done to her. They say once a cheater always a cheater. Well, in this case, it is true for his ass. I turned and walked out of the room to head to my room to get dressed but quickly turned back around. They were already in another make-out session like some got damn teenagers.

"Just so we are clear moms, this nigga will not be attending my wedding today so y'all need to hurry up with y'all little fuck fest so we can head to the venue."

"Son, he is still your father. You can't just cut him out of your life like that. Just give him a chance. He is no longer with his wife anymore."

"He has never been in my life, so I don't need him today so please, leave it alone and don't mention it again. Where is my sister at anyway? She is

48

supposed to be here getting ready and you were supposed to deliver the dress to Sidney like I asked. Did you even do that at least?"

"Your sister offered to take the dress so I and your pops could have some alone time."

I just shook my head then turned and walked out of her room. I knew she was going to try and bring him anyway. Going into my room, I headed to my bathroom and grabbed my dove body wash and towel and jumped in the shower. As I was standing under the water, I couldn't help but think about all the things Sidney has been through behind Sean and now she was getting what she finally deserved. I just hope she goes for it. I had everything in place for the day and her parents should be arriving at our house in about an hour or less in a limo that I rented out for them today to get to the venue. The water started to get a little cold, so I hurried and washed my ass and jumped out. I wrapped the towel around my waist and walked in my room to see my sperm donor sitting at my desk. I just walked around my room and got everything I needed out the dresser and the closet and walked back into the bathroom. As I was getting dressed, I guess my father wasn't done trying to explain his self, so he came to my bathroom door.

"Look son, I know I wasn't there for you but I wanna be here for you now. I have filed for divorce from my wife and it will be finalized in about umm, I want to say ten more days. I know you hate me, but I just want to make it up to you and your sister. I really am sorry for everything I did to your mother and you kids. I hope you can forgive me."

I was sitting there listening to him apologize and maybe he was for real this time. I really wanted it to work this out and he be in all of our lives. If mom can forgive him maybe I can. I opened the bathroom door up and looked at my pops; he was holding some papers in his hands. I was guessing maybe they were his divorce papers.

"Look pops, I can try as long as you are for real about this divorce and you don't hurt my mom again like you did when my sister was born. What're those in your hand?"

"These are my divorce papers and I will do everything I can to make it up to y'all. I promise."

"Aiight, you can start by getting ready for tonight. You will be there when I get married to my girl, so you need to go find a tux so we can do this."

"Let me get out of here and go get one. What time will it start?"

"It starts at 8 pm. Be there on time pops this is your one and only chance to be there for me and if you fuck this up, I will never give you another chance."

He turned and walked out of the room but before he walked completely out, he turned and said, "I love you, son."

I turned back to look in the mirror and smiled. Maybe this would be perfect after all. I tied my tie up and then grabbed my vest and put it on and then went to sit and place my shoes on my feet. Just sitting here thinking about what I was about to do tonight had me nervous as hell. What if she didn't want to get married so soon? What if she didn't want to marry me at all because she feared that I would want to marry her since the baby wasn't really mine?

"Son, she will love what you are doing for her. Stop worrying. I know I talk a lot of shit, but it is just to make you laugh. Now, your father should be back in ten minutes then we can head out. Are we riding in your car or we have to drive our own cars?"

"Actually, Ma, we are riding in a limo so don't trip."

"Ok baby."

She turned and walked out, and I was left there to be in my own thoughts. I must have been that into my thoughts that I didn't hear my pops or my mom calling my name until they were both shaking me trying to get my attention.

"Damn, why y'all shaking me like that?"

"We been talking to you for the last five minutes son," my mom said to me like I really knew that they were talking to me.

I shook my head, stood up, then walked out of the room heading down the stairs with them on my heels like they didn't know what time it was. Walking out the door, the limo was pulling up and I was ready to get this over with, so I can call Sidney my wife. She will be my mines before our little bundle of joy gets here. The driver of the limo jumped out and opened the door and we all climbed in the limo headed to the destination.

Chapter 7

Sidney

J was walking around the house after Cameron left for football practice rubbing my stomach. I was starting to get a small bump and was loving everything about this baby. I wasn't going to let what its father did to me stop me from loving it. It's not the baby's fault that its father was an asshole and raped me and that is how it is here to begin with. Patience is here with Kareem to sit with me because I know Cameron is worried about me, but I didn't want him to be because I am fine. I have to live with what has happened to me and I'm fine with that. There was a knock at the door bringing me out of my thoughts.

Knock, knock…

Getting up and walking to the door to see who it was, I looked out the peephole. Seeing that it was Cameron's sister I opened the door for her, and she had bags in her hand from David's Bridal. One looked like it was a dress in a bag. I was looking at her sideways because I didn't know what she had a dress bag for. She was laughing as she walked in.

"Chey, what you doing here and with this stuff from David's Bridal?"

"Girl, here. Take this and there are your instructions in there. I'm not to tell you nothing else. Oh, Patience and Kareem, I have bags in my car for you guys and your babies as well. Follow me please Kareem. Sidney, I will see you later about 7:30. I will be back."

With that, she turned and walked out the door with Kareem following her. I turned around and walked up to the room Cameron and I shared and laid everything on the bed. As I was looking through the bags, one bag had shoes in it, so I took the shoes out the bag and they were the exact pair I had just been looking at on the website the other day, but I didn't think anybody knew because I was here alone when I looked it up. They were the Embellished Satin Block Heel Sandals. There was also the Dominique satin and lace torsolette bra, with the Dominique lace bikini set. The garter belt I wanted was the "Mrs. And Your Next" garter set was also in one of the bags with the Cathedral length veil with a beaded metallic edge. As I looked in the other bag that the dress was in a letter fell out when I was pulling the dress out. I was now crying because this also was the dress I had told my parents that I want to go try on. It was a ruffled organza plus size mermaid wedding dress. The color of it was white just like I wanted it to be. There was a knock on the door just as I was picking up the letter.

Knock, knock...

"Come in."

"Girl, if you don't stop that damn crying and get dressed. Read your note," Patience laughed.

She turned and walked out while closing the door behind her. I sat on the bed and picked the note up that fell out of the bag. Looking over it, it was from Cameron.

Wifey,

I saw that you were looking at the wedding dress and things the other day when you thought I wasn't home yet, so I sent everything to my sister and my mom to go and get the stuff you wanted. I haven't looked at it because I know its bad luck to see you in your dress before the wedding. Today, you will become my wife; that's if you say yes. I'm hoping that things go as I planned. Yes, yo, nigga can be sneaky just to set this up. Don't worry about anything. It is all taking care of so get dressed and be ready by 7:30 because a limo will be there to pick all of you guys up. I love you and see you at the altar.

Cameron (your husband-to-be)

As I read through the letter he wrote, I began to cry. But I was also wondering, if he didn't see the dress, how did he know what one to get? I picked up the phone to call Chey. It rang twice before she picked it up.

"What's up, sis-in-law? What you need? You are supposed to be getting dressed not calling me."

"I just have a quick question. How did Cameron know what dress to get if he never looked at it?"

"Girl, he had me and mama check your history while y'all was out one day to the doctors for the baby."

"Ok, thank you. Let me get dressed."

She hung up the phone without even saying bye. I walked into the bathroom to get in the shower again before I got dressed. As I climbed in, I was deep in my thoughts wondering if this was too soon and if at some point he may decide to walk away because the baby isn't his. I know y'all be tired of hearing that but shit, its real life right now. I worry about that, but I also worry about me one waking up and the baby that I love may even come out looking like it's no good daddy. The water was starting to get cold, so I hurried up and washed up then hopped out the shower. Wrapping my towel around my body, I walked into the room and began to get dressed. After I was done, there was another knock on the door.

Knock, knock…

"Come in."

"Awww! Hey baby girl. You are so beautiful. But here, I got you something old, something new, something borrowed and something blue. I know you are surprised to see me already but me and your father are here along with all your bridesmaids."

"Umm, mom? Who are my bridesmaids because I never told anyone who would be my bridesmaids."

"Sherry, Lori, Kim, and Pam are. Now, let's finish you up here. Sherry, come start on the makeup and Lori, come on and do this chile's head so we can head out. Oh yeah, Kim is working on that chile head downstairs and Pam is cutting that young man's head. Oh my God! Them beautiful ass babies look so adorable, too."

She turned and walked out of the room and the ladies walked in with their cases to do my hair and makeup. I sat in the chair I had set up in the room over by the window. They each started setting up. Lori pulled out the cape and wrapped it around me and then began to start on my hair while Sherry did some light makeup because they know I hate wearing that anyway. They were both done within twenty minutes. I looked at my hair and makeup and Lori had flat ironed my hair and it was looking good, so I placed the veil on then turned and slipped my shoes on and walked out the room with them walking out behind me. As I walked downstairs, I saw Kareem in a nice ass tux. It was a Vera Wang black notch lapel and Patience had on an off-the-shoulder faille mermaid gown. The babies were all dressed up really cute and my mom and pops were looking good. The bridesmaids were all in the dresses I would have chosen as well. Man, I could go on and on about the dresses, but I won't bore y'all with all that. As I was looking around the house, I noticed that Chey was back as well looking all cute, too.

"Awwww! Look at you, Sidney. You look so beautiful in your wedding dress," Chey acknowledged.

"Thank you, Chey. Is it time to go yet? I'm so nervous and anxious."

"Alright then. Let's go. The limo is pulling up now."

We all walked out and there was a Hummer limo pulling up. I looked on in amazement and walked over as the limo driver got out and helped us all in. There was champagne for those that could drink. After the last person got in, the driver got back in and pulled off towards wherever we were going.

Thirty minutes later…

We pulled up to the Overland Park conventional center and there were cars everywhere. This man done went all out and invited everyone out to our special day and I was geeked. The door to the limo opened and we all climbed out. My dad and mom had helped me out and inside. Walking into the venue, I looked around and was amazed at how Cameron had the placed decorated. I heard music playing softly and knew it was just about time. My ladies got in line; Pam was first, then Kim, then Sherry, and last was Lori. My mom walked inside to go have a seat. Patience and Kareem also walked inside to have a seat. And then next thing I heard was the music for the ladies to walk down the aisle to.

Love
So many things I've got to tell you
but I'm afraid I don't know how
cause there's a possibility you'll look at me differently
Love
Ever since the first moment I spoke your name
From then on, I knew that by you being in my life
Things were destined to change cause……

The ladies were now at the alter standing side by side and then my music came on for me to walk down the aisle and I was so nervous to even start to walk. But my father grabbed my hand and we began to walk down the aisle as I saw Cameron in his white tux. My eyes began to water.

Girl, I'll still kiss your head in the morning

Make you breakfast in bed while you're yawning
and I don't do everything, how you want it
but you can't say your man don't be on it

The song continued to play as I was getting closer. By this time, the tears were streaming down my face uncontrollably.

'cause I know true love ain't easy
Girl, I know it's you,
'cause you complete me
and I just don't want you to leave me,
even though I give you reasons…

I was finally at the altar and as I was looking at Cameron, I could see he was also crying as well. The pastor was finally ready to speak as Cameron and we were staring in each other's eyes.

"Dearly beloved, we are gathered here today in the presence of these witnesses, to join Cameron Hill and Sidney Smith in Matrimony commended to be honorable among all: and therefore, is not to be entered into lightly but reverently, passionately, lovingly and solemnly. Into this-these two persons present now come to be joined. If any person can show just cause why they may not be joined together- let them speak now or forever hold their peace."

There was silence for a brief moment as everyone looked around to make sure nobody spoke up and said anything. Then the pastor continued.

"Who gives this woman to be wed?"

"I do," my father stated.

He handed my hand over to Cameron and went to have a seat next to my mother.

"Let us all bow our heads for prayer. Dear Heavenly Father, our hearts are filled with great happiness on Cameron and Sidney's wedding day, as they come before you pledging their hearts and lives to one another. Grant that they may be ever true and loving, living together in such a way as to never bring shame or heartbreak into their marriage. Temper their hearts with kindness and understanding, rid them of all pretense of jealousy. Help them to remember to be each other's sweetheart, helpmate, friend and guide, so that together they may meet the cares and problems of life more bravely and with the passage of time, may the home they are creating today, truly be a place of love, and harmony, where your spirit is ever present. Bless this union we pray and walk beside Cameron and Sidney throughout all their lives together. We ask these things in Jesus name; Amen."

"Amen."

"Marriage is perhaps the greatest and most challenging adventure of human relationships. No ceremony can create your marriage; only you can do that through love and patience; through dedication and perseverance; through talking and listening, helping and supporting and believing in each other; through tenderness and laughter; through learning to forgive, learning to appreciate your differences, and by learning to make the important things matter, and to let go of the rest. What this ceremony can do is witness and affirms the choice you make to stand together as life mates and partners."

Man, these tears just keep on flowing as I stand here looking in Cameron's eyes. All I saw was love. The pastor speaking brought me out my thoughts.

"Repeat after me; I, Cameron, take you Sidney, to be my wife. To have and to hold from this day forward, for better or worse, for richer, for poorer, in sickness and in health, to love and to cherish; from this day forward until death do us part.

Cameron repeated his vows. The tears just were flowing all down my face as he was confessing his love to me in his words through our vows.

"Now Sidney, repeat after me; I, Sidney, take you, Cameron, to be my husband. To have and to hold from this day forward, for better or worse, for richer, for poorer, in sickness and in health, to love and to cherish; from this day forward until death do us part."

I began to look into Cameron's eyes confessing my love to him through my vows as these tears just kept coming down.

"Rings please."

The best man handed the ring to the pastor. And the pastor handed me the ring to place on Cameron's hand.

"OK, repeat after me, Sidney. I, Sidney, give you Cameron, this ring as an eternal symbol of my love and commitment to you."

I placed the ring on Cameron's ring finger and repeated after the pastor. The pastor then gave Cameron my ring to place on my hand.

"Now Cameron, repeat after me; I, Cameron, give you Sidney, this ring as an eternal symbol of my love and commitment to you."

Cameron placed my ring on my ring finger and repeated the pastor. As he did, I began to feel butterflies in my stomach that I have never felt before. It was either the baby moving or the love between us just caused butterflies.

"Wedding rings serve as the symbol of the covenant you have just spoken. They are the outward and visible sign of an inward and invisible love which binds your hearts together. As they are of the finest of earth's materials, so your love is of the richest of spiritual values. As rings are without edge or seam, having no beginning and no end, they symbolize the perfection of a love that cannot end. Let us pray. Bless these rings, O God, to be the visible sign of the vows here made, that each who gives a ring and each who wears one may be reminded of their promises, evermore living and growing in the spirit of your love. Amen."

"Amen."

"Join me as we ask God's blessing on this new couple. Eternal Father, redeemer, we now turn to you, and as the first act of this couple in their newly formed union, we ask you to protect their home. May they always turn to you for guidance, for strength, for provisions and direction. May they glorify you in the choices they make, in the ministries they involve themselves in, and in all that they do. Use them to draw others to yourself, and let them stand as a testimony to the world of your faithfulness. We ask this in Jesus name, amen."

"Amen"

"By the power vested in me, by the state of Missouri, I now pronounce you husband and wife. You may now kiss the bride." Cameron leaned in and gave me the most passionate kiss ever. "I present to you, Mr. and Mrs. Hill."

We turned around as the broom was placed behind us so we could jump the broom. We jumped and began to walk back down the aisle. As we walked out hand in hand, I was feeling like this was the best day of my life. I looked up at Cameron and he had this big ass smile on his face. I've never seen his smile reach his eyes this high since when first got together. I was loving it though.

"Babe, this is the happiest day of my life and I thank you for surprising me with this wedding. I really appreciate everything you have been doing for me. I'm glad that you did this. Now I know you won't leave me when this baby comes. Ha ha ha."

"Girl, you know I wasn't going anywhere anyway. You mine and I'm yours till death do us part wifey."

This man is always doing something, but I was loving it. I heard music playing and I turned to look at him like, "what the hell is going on now?" Cameron started laughing as he pulled me into where the reception was being held and everyone was walking in already then, I heard the DJ announce us as we were walking in.

"Thank you for all coming out to celebrate the union of Mr. Cameron hill and Mrs. Sidney Hill. This song is for you guys as you guys have your first dance as husband and wife.

What would I do without your smart mouth
Drawing me in, and you kicking me out

Lovely Ann

Got my head spinning, no kidding, I can't pin you down
What's going on in that beautiful mind
I'm on your magical mystery ride…

We slow danced to the song that was playing and we enjoyed ourselves the entire night. From dancing to cutting the cake, to speeches, father-daughter dancing and everything else. We laughed and had a grand time like what was going on with us all didn't even matter at this time.

Chapter 8

Lucas

Yep, it's your boy Lucas from Loving a Kansas City King. Lovely Ann decided to bring me out. Well, shit. She didn't have a choice because me and my crew was appearing anyway. Whether she liked it or not. We came on the scene to help Cameron and Sidney with this cat name Sean who liked to put his hands on women. Me and my crew ain't for that shit. This man beat two women and raped the both of them and he was gonna pay. Let me take you back to the day where we beat that nigga and killed his ass.

Two months ago, ...

We had walked into this man house searching all over for Sidney and his ass. We found Sidney in a room naked, tied up to the bed crying and praying that somebody come and save her. I had Cameron go get her and take her out of here. Me and my crew continued to search the house till we came to a room where the door was closed. We opened the door quietly and this nigga was laying in the bed sleep; he didn't even move when we came into the room. I walked up to him and placed my gun to his head. That's when he jumped up quick as fuck.

"What the fuck! Who the fuck are you and what are you doing in my house?"

"Nigga, don't worry about it. Get your ass up now."

This nigga thought he had a choice, but he had another thing coming.

We forced him to get up and he tried to fight Trent, so Trent shot his ass in his leg. Then Mason and Snoop dragged his ass to the car and placed him in the trunk.

"Yo' Cameron, you sure you don't want in on this man?"

"Naw, that's not my thing. Y'all gone head and have at it."

I nodded and got in my whip along with everyone else and peeled out.

We headed to our warehouse where we tortured people. It took us about twenty minutes to get there. Soon as we pulled up, we all hopped out while Trent and Mason dragged this nigga Sean inside then took him to the room with the steel table in it. They strapped him on as I was walking inside. He was squirming trying to get out but there was no way possible he was going to get free from those straps.

"Sean, buddy. There is no way you can get free from your restraints so you might as well stop. Now, we are here because you decided you were going to kidnap and rape my homie's girl in front of him and you also, like beating on people so yo' time is up. Any last words?"

"Fuck you bitch. That bitch deserved it. Both them bitches did."

I walked over and grabbed the things I needed as everyone else walked out. They knew what was about to happen. I flipped the switch and the table turned to a standing position. A hat fell down towards his head and I placed it on then strapped it on as I walked back over to flip the second switch. His ass started shaking as the electric shock went through his body. He died in a matter of ten minutes from it. Yes, a nigga likes to use electric shock to kill people that deserve that shit. I didn't give a fuck! Shit, y'all niggas know this.

Present day...

We were standing around watching this beautiful wedding and reception of Cameron and Sidney and you could just feel the love between the both of them. I was just happy for my boy. He finally found the one to make him settle down. Cameron had been fucking this chick and that chick for the longest but soon as he met Sidney, things changed. But I'm happy he finally got what I have with Olivia. Olivia was now 8 months pregnant with our daughter. We already have two sons but now we are expecting our 3rd child. Looking over at the crew, at Olivia and the ladies, everyone was happy these days. Trent and Brooklyn were still having issues conceiving but they were not letting that bring them down. Snoop and Kaylee were actually still engaged and are planning to be married next year. Mason and Mia were now on baby number 3 as well and they have gotten married about six months ago. Mia still goes to therapy but she has accepted the fact that Miracle couldn't be here with them. Snoop and Trent walked over to me as I was watching everybody.

"Nigga, why you over staring at all of us like some type of creep," Trent joked like always.

"Nigga, I'm just watching everything and just happy that we all are in a good place now."

"Fool, you just happy you can lay up under Olivia. Especially while you keep getting her ass pregnant. Every time after, she has one not even 3 months later, she pregnant again! Shit, yo' son Lamont is only 11 months old and Lucas Jr is two."

"Lyric is going to be spoiled, watch and see. Her mama already got her room looking like Pepto Bismol. She won't even let me go in there and touch anything or set anything up."

They started laughing and then walked off. After they were gone, Olivia waddled over to me and hugged me then stepped up on her tippy toes to give me a kiss. So, I grabbed her ass as she kissed me.

"What you doing over here baby?"

"Just looking at how happy everybody is and how far we came since Lucas Jr was born."

Olivia nodded while she sat down at the table then took a sip of water and started eating a little of her food. Everybody walked over and sat at the table and began to dig in their food. Just sitting here looking at how happy everybody was, was just amazing and I was here for it. I'm glad I made the decisions that I made when everything went down and even when I turned everything over to Snoop and Mason. I have my own club called Lucas' Lounge. It has been doing well these days and I was all for it.

"OK, all single ladies. Please come on and gather around."

Kaylee jumped up and went on over with everybody else while Sidney stood there with her bouquet to throw to the ladies. Next thing you know, as she threw the bouquet, Kaylee pushed people out the way and she caught it. She plays dirty when it comes to competition. I shook my head and sat there and just waited around. We sat around and had a good time for another hour and then we all headed out right after Cameron and

Sidney left and went to the airport. I was sending them to Jamaica for their honeymoon. It was the least I could do as a gift to them for their wedding. Walking to my car, I opened the door so Olivia could get in. As she was starting to get in, she doubled over in pain. Right then and there, I knew it was time to head to the hospital. She couldn't be coming early; she still had a few more weeks left to bake in there. I was running around like crazy because I was nervous again like I always get when she goes into labor.

After a few minutes of the pain, Olivia stood straight up and as she did, there was a gush of liquid that came shooting out between her legs. I knew it was her water breaking. I helped her in the car and yelled to the family to meet us at the hospital and that it was time. I then ran to the driver's side of the car and hopped in and sped away towards Research Medical Center. It took me about ten minutes to get there. Normally, it would take twenty minutes or so, but I had to hurry and get my baby to the hospital. I pulled up to the emergency entrance and hopped out. I ran inside to get a doctor or nurse to help me. A nurse walked up with a wheelchair and followed me out to the car and we helped Olivia out where they wheeled her up to labor and delivery. As we got on the elevator, I was nervous and excited all at the same time to meet my little princess Lyric.

"Aghhhhhh, fuck! Lucas, I hate you for doing this to me again! I'm not having any more of yo' nappy head ass babies. I can't take this pain anymore! After this, give me some damn pain meds dammit."

"Honey, we will give you some soon as we get to the room, but you have to keep calm and breathe for me, ok sweetie?"

We got off the elevator and I couldn't do shit but laugh at her ass cause she thought she was having a natural birth, but she couldn't because she has already had 2 C-Sections, so she was having another one.

"Aye, she is having another C-section so there ain't no need for y'all to give the pain meds. She needs to be going to the room where y'all do the C-section."

"Ok, you will have to change into this and then we will all head to the OR. Ms. Olivia, I need you to put this gown on and get in bed. We will be right back to prep you for your C-section."

The nurse turned and walked out of the room as I helped Olivia into the hospital gown. After helping her into it, I put on the scrubs the nurse handed me. We sat there and waited for the nurse to come back into the room to get us for this C-Section so we can meet our little princess Lyric. We waited for about ten to twenty minutes before someone finally decided to come to the room.

Knock...knock...

In walked the doctor with a smile on her face like she knew that the baby was coming soon. I just shook my head cause I knew Olivia was bout to be with the shits as always. She hated hospitals and not only that, the doctor walked in smiling while Olivia was in so much pain.

"So, it looks like it's time for baby girl. Are we ready?" the doctor asked a stupid ass question.

"What the hell you think? I been ready for her ass to get out of here so I can have my body back. That was a real stupid ass question anyway," Olivia replied back.

"Well, the nurse will be in shortly to come and get you all and take you down to the OR," the doctor contorted.

Without giving us time to reply, she turned and walked out of the room. We sat around talking till the nurses came in and were getting everything together. I was excited to see my baby girl finally.

"Ok, let's get you to the OR sweetheart. It's time to deliver your little bundle of joy," the nurse exclaimed.

They wheeled the bed out the room while I followed right behind them ready and waiting to see my beautiful baby girl. It took us a few minutes to get to the room to have the C-Section. They stopped me at the door and told me one of them will come back out to get me when it is time. They took every bit of thirty minutes for them to come back out and I was getting anxious already.

As I was walking into the room, I saw Olivia laid out on the bed with a sheet covering the top half of her body so she couldn't see what they are doing when they cut her open.

Forty-five minutes later...

As we sat there waiting impatiently for them to deliver the baby, we heard a cry.

"Waaa--- Waaa."

I looked up and the doctor was holding up this beautiful baby girl who was the spitting image of my wife. I was excited to see my baby. The nurse came over to get the baby to clean her up. Then the doctor spoke again.

"Umm, you guys? We have another baby coming."

"I should have known considering this nigga is a twin," Olivia replied.
"Ha ha ha," I laughed.
As we sat there and waited for the doctor to tell us what the baby is, I was really hoping for another girl because we already have two boys.
"It's another girl," the doctor exclaimed.
"Yasss! We got another girl," I said with excitement.
The doctor held the baby up so I could see her, and she was also the spitting image of her mother. They both looked like Olivia so maybe they were identical twins. I kissed my wife on the cheek and thanked her for giving me these beautiful blessings. I was thinking of a name that went with Lyric and I decided on Lyrica, but I wanted to run it by Olivia first.
"So, Olivia. I was thinking of a name and I came up with Lyrica. What you think?" I asked her.
"I actually like that. It goes perfectly with Lyric. Lyrica and Lyric, I love them," Olivia replied.
She began to look tired, so I kissed her and walked over to where the babies were. I was so happy looking down at them. The nurses finished cleaning them up and told me she was taking them to the nursery to be weighed and give them their first bath. She wrapped one baby up and another nurse wrapped the other baby. Walking back over to where Olivia was, the nurses showed the girls to us and Olivia started tearing up.
"We have twin girls Lucas. I can't believe I was pregnant and never knew we were having twins," Olivia cried as she gave the girls a kiss.
The nurses turned and walked back to lay the babies in the plastic crib then rolled them out.
"Baby, I'm going after the girls I will see you when you get out of here."
"Ok, baby. Watch out for our girls. I love you husband," Olivia replied.
I leaned down and kissed her lips passionately then stood up and walked out towards where the nurses were and to my little princesses. As I was walking towards the nursery, I sent out a massive text to the family to let them all know that we had twins instead of one baby. I should have known sooner or later it was going to be twins considering that I'm also one.
One week later…
We were now home, and I was exhausted; these twins were a handful.

When one was sleeping the other was up crying. I just wish that they would get on the same page because we were running on low fuel. Who would have ever thought that having twins would be so fucking hard. I needed a break from the wife and the kids, so I headed out to my club to go check on things. Yes, that's right. Instead of being in the streets like I used to, I now have a club of my own. I only step in when I need to. Getting in my Impala SS, I headed to my club. I was pulling up in no time. Climbing out the car, I headed inside. The club was jumping as I walked in and the music was blasting through the speakers.

It's 2:30 in the morning
'Round this time, you know we going in, yeah
I have the key, so you don't throw it in, no
But you get crazy when you're horny
I feel like I should be your lover, I should be your friend

As I walked up to the bar, there was this fine ass chick sitting there so I decided to walk up and introduce myself. I know what y'all thinking but shit, I needed to get out and meet new people for the time being. It ain't cheating if I'm just talking right?

"Hi there. I'm Lucas, the owner if this club. I just wanted to introduce myself to you. I saw a sexy woman sitting over here by her lonesome self and I had to come put a smile on that nice beautiful face," I flirted.

"Well, hello Mr. Lucas. I'm Lonzia," she flirted back, with a smile on her face.

We were smiling and having a nice conversation until I looked down at my phone and saw that it almost 1 am. I had to hurry and get home.

"Look, Lonzia. I enjoyed talking to you, but I have to get home before all hell breaks loose. My wife would be tripping if I'm not home at a real decent hour considering I'm a married man," I sighed.

I know y'all wondering what I was up to but shit, like I said, it ain't cheating if it's just conversation. I stood up and hugged her. I felt like my wife was watching me as I hugged Lonzia. I looked around but didn't see her anywhere. Pulling away from Lonzia, I grabbed my keys and phone then looked down to see I had 2 missed calls from my wife and a voicemail. I decided not to listen to the voicemail or call her back since I was headed home anyway. Lonzia grabbed my phone out my hand and went to typing I'm guessing she was putting her number in my phone but there was no way I was going to be calling her like I said I'm married but I may get somebody for her though.

65

"Here is my number. Use it if you need to get away or talk. I'm here, no strings attached," Lonzia confessed.

"Look, Lonzia. You are a nice girl and all, but I can't do this, but I may have somebody for you though. I got a homie name Jacques I can introduce you to but as far as me and you, there can't be nothing but friendship. It was nice talking to you, but I got to get going and head home to my wife and kids," I confessed.

I turned and walked away. As I was walking to my car, I sent Jacques a text with ol' girl number to let him know he should hit her up and shoot his shot. I hopped in my SS and pulled off.

Look, said I was getting' some head, get-getting some head
Ran down on a bitch, she almost pissed on her leg
Bitches think they fuckin' with me, must be sick in the head
Why don't you chill with the beef and get some chicken instead
Got the crown, and shut it down, have them hype up in the 6

I was cruising through the streets blasting the radio as Hot 103 Jamz was playing one of Cardi B's songs. Pulling up to my crib, I pulled in to the garage and climbed out the car then went inside. As I did, I heard one of y'all ladies newest anthem's playing throughout the house so I knew it was bout to be some shit. Especially when I heard my wife singing her heart out like she was really feeling the song.

You tell me you love me
But I ain't feeling it lately
You say your love keeping me fly but
Can't keep me from looking' so crazy
Come in at 6 in the mornin'

As I got closer to our room, I heard sniffles. I knew I felt her watching me at the club. I had to make this right with her. Walking closer, Olivia really started singing her heart out, looking me in my eyes as she sang.

How would you like it if I do the things that you do
put you on do not disturb and entertain these dudes
I'mma ride him crazy and you'll never have a clue
Give another guy what belongs to you
I'mma call up Brian, I'mma facetime Ryan
I'mma text Lorenzo and Imma leave you crying
Don't get it twisted I can play this game too
How would you like it if I do the same to you, (same to you, yeah)

I walked over to her and Olivia slapped the dog shit out of me as soon as

I touched her. Now I was pissed because she didn't even let me explain. Shit, I didn't even do anything. I just had a fucking conversation with this chick, nothing more.

"Look, Olivia. I don't put my hands on you so don't put your fucking hands on me. Now you mad for what cause you saw me talking to a chick and hug her when I left? Shit, I passed her number off to the homie Jacques. I told her I was married. What more will it take for you to get that you got me for life, and I wouldn't cheat on you again. After the first and last time, I never cheated on you. Come on, ma. Now turn this bullshit ass song off and come give your husband a hug," I yelled, pissed that she even would even think I would do some bullshit like that.

"Nigga, fuck you! Go sleep in the guest room tonight. I need to be by myself. I can't believe you were entertaining another bitch. How would you like it if I would have done you the same way?" Olivia yelled back at me.

Instead of continuing to argue, I just walked out of the room and went to my man cave. I walked down and poured me a shot of Hen then sat down and rolled me a blunt as I sat and thought about everything that transpired tonight.

Chapter 9

Patience

W atching Sidney and Cameron get married put me in my feelings because that used to be my nigga. I mean, I love Kareem and everything, but I still loved Cameron, but he is Sidney's now and I had to let that go. I was walking around the house with Khalilah trying to get her to go to sleep. She was a bit cranky so I walked to her room with a warm bottle for her hoping that would help calm her down. I sat in the rocking chair to feed her. While I was doing that, she started falling asleep.

"Khalilah, baby girl. I'm going to be here every step of the way for you. I know I'm not your biological mother, but I would love to adopt you and make things more permanent soon as me and your father get married. I won't ever take your mother's place, but I would like to fill that void for you and your father."

I looked up and saw Kareem looking at me with tears in his eyes. I knew then he heard what I was saying to lil' mama.

"Babe, you know you have been everything since I brought her home and when her mom passed. I would be honored for you to adopt Khaliah, but we don't have to wait till we get married; we can go do it this week. We can go down to the courthouse and file the petition tomorrow before I go back to work at the hospital. I'm very proud of the mother and the person you have become since the beating from your ex," Kareem acknowledged.

I took the bottle out the baby mouth and replaced it with her pacifier. I burped her then placed her down in her crib and wrapped the blanket around her small body like a burrito. We walked out of the room and I walked towards Alyssa room to go check on her. As I walked in, I saw that she was standing up in her crib trying to climb out as usual.

"Alyssa Marie, get your little butt down now," I told her.

She jumped when she heard my voice but also started laughing when she saw that me and Kareem saw that she was trying to climb out of her crib. I walked over, picked her up, then went to make her a warm bottle of milk with cereal in it. They say it helps babies sleep and since she was 3 months, I have been putting cereal in her bottles and it worked. We walked back towards her room where I sat in her rocking chair and gave her the bottle. Alyssa began to fall asleep instantly as usual. As soon as she finished the bottle, I went and laid her down in her crib then walked out her room; shutting her door and turning the light on but making sure her nightlight was on. We walked into our room and I went to shower. I know I never said anything to Kareem when he said we can go down to the courthouse tomorrow, but he knew when he was ready then so was I. Hopping in the shower, I washed up at least two times before getting out. I wrapped my towel around my body and walked into the room and grabbed my lotion then sat on the bed to lotion my body.

"Kareem, baby. Don't think I didn't hear you earlier because I did. I want you to do it at your pace. We don't have to rush because I know you still grieving for your baby mother. I'm ready whenever you are so if you wanna go tomorrow we can," I told Kareem, meaning every word I said.

"I know baby and I'm ready to do this. It's been a few since she died and I'm starting to accept things for how they are. I'm ready for you to adopt Khalilah and be the mother that she will need. Plus, we can get started on me adopting Alyssa, too since her no good ass daddy signed over his rights. Oh yeah! Before I get in the shower, you need to start planning our wedding, too," Kareem stated in a matter of fact tone.

I guess daddy has spoken. He turned and walked to the bathroom and went to get in the shower. I went to my dresser and put on this nice, red, sexy lingerie and sat in the middle of the bed till Kareem came out of the bathroom. Soon as he walked out with his towel wrapped around his lower half, I motioned for him to come to me as I crawled to the edge of the bed. As soon as he came, I pulled the towel from around his waist. I dropped that towel and began to go to work on giving my man some of the best head that he has ever had.

"Ssssss—shit, girl! Suck that dick mama. Fuck," Kareem moaned out.

I went to work on his balls, and he was enjoying every bit of it. He started pumping into my mouth and I knew he was getting ready to cum. I deep throated him and felt his dick touch the back of my throat where he shot his seeds. He picked me up then laid me back and began to suck the soul out of my pussy. I was cumming in no time.

"Aw, fuck baby, I'm cumming already! What the fuck," I moaned out.

"That's because I know what I'm doing when I'm eating that pussy baby. Now you bout give me at least two more nuts before I give you this dope dick. Lay your ass back," Kareem spoke up.

Shit, he didn't have to tell me twice cause I was ready for that fire ass head he gave up. Soon as my head hit the bed, this niggas tongue went to work on my pussy. Kareem began to suck on my clit and no sooner than he did that, he placed a finger in each hole. I was cumming instantly back to back. He climbed up and slowly entered my waiting wet pussy.

"Sssssss, baby! This dick is feeling too damn good," I stated while moaning.

Kareem was taking his time with me making love to my mind body and soul. Next thing I know he was flipping me over and began to beat my pussy up. We both were moaning. I began to clench my pussy around his dick. I had that mothafucka in a tight choke hold and Kareem released his seeds coating my walls.

"Dammit girl! Let my dick go! Shit, fuck! I'm cumming, Ma," he moaned out.

Kareem pulled out and rolled over, all out of breath. We laid there for a few more minutes catching our breath before we both got up to go wash up. Finishing, I went and got one of Kareem's big t-shirts out and put it on. We both climbed in bed and was sleep in no time.

Chapter 10

Cameron

Yep, yo' boy did it. I married the love of my life and it feels so fucking amazing. We were in Jamaica for our honeymoon and we were enjoying ourselves. We have been fucking all over the hotel room and on our private beach. We got a text from Lucas a few weeks ago saying Olivia had the baby and she had twins. We all thought it was one baby but turns out, baby girl was hiding behind her sister. Staring over at my wife, she was sleeping so peacefully with her hand resting on her stomach. My baby was starting to show, she had a small bump. I placed small kisses on her stomach, and I felt the baby move. That was a first. He or she doesn't normally move when I kiss her stomach. As the baby kicked, Sidney laughed at me when I jumped back. I guess that woke her sleepy head ass up.

"Oh, so you think that's funny huh?" I asked her.

"Babe, you should have seen the way you jumped back, though. That shit was funny as fuck," she laughed.

I got something for her though. I went to tickle her sides and between her thighs. Then I saw how good that pussy was looking, and I went in for a taste of that wet shit. As soon as my mouth touched her clit, Sidney started squirming around.

"Ssssss—shit, baby," Sidney moaned.

Just what I liked to hear. I continued to suck the soul outta her ass. That shit was so damn wet, she was cumming back to back. I placed my finger inside her pussy and was fingering her and sucking her. She started squirting all over the place. I lifted her leg up and was devouring that pussy like the monster I was. I placed a finger in her ass also, but I still had one finger in her pussy and sucking on her clit.

"F—fuucck, baby! Yes, I'm cumming! Oh my god," Sid screamed out.

Shit, I was glad we had our own area of the beach house we were staying in right now. I lifted up and slid right on in her tight ass pussy and that shit squeezed the fuck out of my dick. She had my shit in a choke hold and if she didn't let it go soon, I was gonna cum in no time.

"Fuck girl! Quit choking my dick! Let it go Ma or I won't be lasting that long in this shit," I exclaimed.

Sidney finally released the choke hold she had, and I started delivering her ass them long, deep, slow strokes. I knew they would make her start squirting and cumming all over the place.

"Fuck, I'm cumming, daddy," she yelled.

I knew Sidney would after she released, I picked her ass up and walked over to the dresser and sat her ass on the edge and spread her legs open and went back in. I was going to work on her pussy, and she was creaming all over my dick. As I looked down at my pole went in and out that pussy. Damn, I love looking at my pole going in and out that wet shit.

"Sssssss—sshit girl! I'm cumming," I yelled out.

I was coating her walls with my seeds instantly as I saw her creaming all over my dick. I stood there catching my breath as I slid out of her wet shit and let her down off the dresser. I walked her back over to the bed and went to the bathroom to hop in the shower. I turned the water on the temperature of my liking. I washed my body as I so, I felt a cold breeze and I knew Sidney ass was coming to join me in the shower. I rinsed off and no sooner than all the soap was off, Sidney dropped to her knees and began to deep throat my dick.

"Sssss—shit girl! What the fuck," I moaned.

I felt my dick hit the back of her throat and she didn't even gag. I lived for shit like this. My baby was sucking the hell outta my pole. My knees were starting to buckle. I had to grab hold of the shower pole, so I didn't fall and bust my ass. My baby had those skills and I was loving every bit of them. Sidney began to play with my balls as she was deep throating the fuck outta my pole.

"Aw, fuck, girl," I moaned.

I released down her throat. I pulled Sidney up then picked her up and leaned her against the shower wall to fuck the shit out of her ass since she wanted to come in here and play those games sucking my dick like that. She was screaming out of pleasure and four strokes later, I was coating her walls with my seeds. I swear pregnant pussy was the best; it always has me busting quick. I let her down. I held on to Sidney so she could get her balance together, so she wouldn't fall. I grabbed her soap and began to wash her up and we switched sides, so she can rinse her body off and I washed my body again then rinsed off. After we were done washing up, we both got out the shower. We dried off then wrapped the towels around our bodies and walked back into the room to dress and pack so we could head home. I had to get ready for this game we had coming up next week. We had to get back to reality. Sidney had to finish getting her other shop ready to open it should be opening up in another month. She had to hire some more people. She already had Patience working there and she needed a few more beauticians and a few barbers as well. My baby was doing the damn thing all on her own. She had a shop in Kansas and now she has a shop on the Missouri side, too.

2 hours later…

We were walking onto our private jet to head home. I wasn't even ready to go back yet. I was enjoying this away time we got but we do have to get back. The pilot let us know it was time for takeoff, it was no sooner than we took off we were both knocked out. Shit, all that fucking we have been doing, of course, we were tired. We slept for the entire four-hour flight until they were telling us we were landing. I tapped Sidney to wake her cause she still didn't wake up. My baby was sleeping so peacefully.

"Wife, we are home. Let's go so we can get home and get some more rest. We can get back to the real world tomorrow," I stated.

Sidney dragged herself up and we walked off our private jet where we headed to call a yellow cab so we could get home. Why I didn't have my car? Well, I left that bitch at home and we were dropped off in the limo. I should have had my mom or somebody to pick us up, but I didn't want anyone to evade our space right now. As we were walking around to baggage claim to get our luggage, I turned my phone on to see I had tons of notifications come through since I talked to Lucas the other week. I've had my phone off and didn't turn it on till now.

Lucas: *Bruh, I need to talk to you. Man, I fucked up big time with Olivia. Hit me back.*

Lucas: *Come on, bruh! I really need you right now I know you on yo' honeymoon and shit but I really need your help with Olivia before she leaves my ass.*

Lucas: *Man bruh! She said she wanted a divorce. I can't live without her and my kids. I don't want any other woman but Olivia. I met this chick name*

Lonzia the other night at my club. We chopped it up till like 1 to 2 in the morning and when I was getting ready to head home, I hugged her, and she put her number in my phone, but I sent the number to Jacques and deleted her number and Olivia found out by popping up at the club and when I got home, she went in on my ass. Bruh, help me out here man I need you like yesterday. You know I ain't never needed you like this and I ain't one of them soft ass niggas, but I really need yo' help.

Me: *My bad, bruh. I had my phone off while on the honeymoon, but I got you to come by the crib in about thirty mins and we can chop it up.*

I slide my phone back in my pocket and just started shaking my head. Lucas ass was always getting caught up with chicks. I thought he was doing the good thing here these last few years but now he done fucked up again. This nigga was never gonna learn. He was getting caught in these sticky situations. I picked up our last few bags and headed to the entrance where the cab driver should be waiting. Soon as we walked outside the cab driver was there waiting and I placed my bags in the trunk and we got in and headed to the crib. We were pulling up in twenty minutes and soon as we pulled up, Lucas was sitting in the driveway.

"Cam, what is Lucas doing here?" Sidney asked.

"He needs to talk but I shouldn't be long. Go in and shower and lay yo' fine self down and rest," I replied.

We both got out the car and I grabbed the bags and we headed to the door. As I was opening it up, Lucas got out the car and walked up greeting us.

"What's up, y'all? I'm sorry for bothering y'all soon as y'all get back from your honeymoon, but I needed to talk something serious before I lose my family and I ain't tryna lose them at all. I love them too much," Lucas sighed.

I could tell my boy was hurt like hell, so I had to get him back in good graces with Olivia before she divorced his crybaby ass. We all walked into the house and I turned my alarm system off, so these damn people won't be coming or calling thinking someone done broke in this bitch.

"It's cool, Lucas. You helped us out so it's only right that we help you out. How bout this; I go see Olivia while y'all talk about it and then I can see what I can do but I need you to tell me everything that happened so I can put in a good word for you," Sidney told his ass.

Lucas ran everything down to us from the time he got to the club to when he got home and her putting him out the room and now her claiming she filing for divorce come Monday morning. This nigga done fucked up and I hope it was a way we could fix this somehow cause if they didn't make then who's to say there is hope for us? Lucas and Olivia, reminds you of Remy Ma and Pap's relationship. You know, that black love.

"Ok look, babe. You head over to Lucas' crib and let me talk to my man and see what we all can do to get this nigga back in the good graces of his wife," I told Sidney.

She grabbed her keys, gave me a kiss, and then headed out the door. But before she walked out, Sidney turned around and spoke to Lucas one more time.

"You better hope we can help you fix this, but you better be planning something big since you done fucked up big time. You need to understand us women take our vows very seriously and when you break those vows by entertaining the next bitch, that's like a slap in the fucking face. I feel where she is coming from, but I also feel for her because this is the ultimatum betrayal that you could have ever done. Not just that but she did just give birth to twins for yo' ass. Now let me get the fuck outta here before I be cussing yo' ass out for her," Sidney fussed, walking out the door.

"Nigga, you done pissed her off. Now if I don't get none for a while imma kick yo' ass," I laughed at Lucas' expense.

"Man, look bruh. I am confused about all this shit. I ain't never been married before. I don't know the dos or don'ts in marriage. Who knew that me having a conversation with another chick would cause all this drama between me and my wife? Mannnn," Lucas cried as he held his head in his hands.

"Look Lucas, now that y'all are married you got to understand that you cannot hug or kiss another chick; if yo' wife sees it or not. All hell is gonna break loose. To them, you done cheated on them. Some women don't think like that but in yo' case, your wife feels like you disrespected her and cheated on her basically even if you feel like you didn't, she feels like you did. Olivia isn't secure in y'all marriage because of the past and you have to fix that. Maybe y'all should do some marriage counseling. It could do you guys some good," I informed Lucas.

"Man, I'mma street nigga. What I look like going to see a therapist about my marital issues with my wife?" Lucas yelled.

"Look, if you wanna fix yo' marriage you gonna put in the time and effort for what you really care about. Let's look up some marriage counselors," I responded back.

"Man, I don't want to do therapy, but I guess I have to since I'm the reason why she feels the way she does anyway," Lucas revealed.

Lovely Ann

We sat around and waited for Sidney to call or text to let us know the play on her end. While waiting for Sidney, I did some research for Lucas and wrote a few addresses, names, and numbers down so they can call them and
Set something up.

Chapter 11

Sidney

J was pissed at Lucas for what he did to Olivia knowing that girl loved his dirty draws. But not only that, she just gave birth to 2 of his big-headed ass babies. These niggas always think they have it good and wanna have their cake and eat it to. Olivia was sitting crying her eyes out over what Lucas did and she was really talking about divorcing him.

"Look, Olivia, you gotta stop crying girl. You love that man and y'all are gonna fix this. How about you think about going to marriage counseling and fix you guy's relationship before you jump to divorce? I asked.

"I want to work this out, but I don't know if I can trust him. I what if he does it again but this time he actually sleeps with her?" Olivia cried on my shoulder.

"If he wants to fix this will you be open to it?" I replied.

"I guess I can try but he has to be. You know how these hood niggas act. They feel like hood niggas don't need a therapist to get involved in their relationships," Olivia confessed. I picked up my phone and texted Cameron to let him know.

Me: *She agreed to marriage counseling so get a therapist to see them ASAP.*

Cameron: *I'm on it bae. Thank you. Now calm down and don't stress my baby out woman.*

I placed my phone in my purse and sat with Olivia a little bit longer till I
got her to calm down some so I could head home and get some rest.
Olivia was lying on the couch finally sleep so I went to check on her
kids before I left.
All four of them were asleep. I was bout to head home but as I was
leaving, Lucas came in. I didn't say shit to him 'cause I was still pissed at
his ass. Hitting my alarm on my ride, I hopped in my car and headed home.
I got to the house in no time. Walking inside the house I went straight to
our room and Cameron was in there waiting for me.
"I got a bath ran for you so go ahead and get in and relax,"
Cameron confessed.
This man was being so sweet, and I was loving every bit of it. Who knew
I would fall in love again and with a football player at that? I walking
into the bathroom to see he had rose petals in the tub and candles lit all
over the bathroom. I looked around in amazement and tears started to
spill out my eyes. This baby had me so emotional and I was over
these emotions already. I couldn't wait till I had this damn baby.
Cameron walked into the bathroom and looked at me and began to wipe
my face and helped me undress and climb in the tub. As I sat in the tub I
laid back and relaxed. Cameron turned and walked out of the bathroom
and left me to relax. As I was sitting in the tub, I began to think
about everything I've been through my entire life and I'm glad that I
met Cameron when I did. Sean caused me a lot of pain and suffering
and I'm glad that he can never hurt me again. He gave me a precious
gift and I'm going to love him or her for the rest of my life. As I sat
back relaxing in the tub, I closed my eyes and got even more comfortable.
I must have dozed off because I jumped up as soon as Cameron
burst through the bathroom door.
"What the hell you busting in the bathroom like that for boy?" I asked.
"Shit, yo' ass been in here for damn near an hour. I was coming to check
on you. Good thing I did because your ass was knocked the fuck out.
Hurry up and wash yo' funky ass. Get out and come to bed. We have a
long day tomorrow," Cameron replied.
I nodded and began to let the water out while hopping in the shower to
wash my body off. I'm glad Cameron did come in when he did because
I probably would have been there all night. I swear I'm always fucking

tired. But he is right; I do have a long day tomorrow. I have ten interviews,
I have to pick out the furniture for the shop, and pick out the colors.
It's going to be one hell of a day. Good thing I will have Patience with me
to help out. Thinking of Patience, I'm very proud of her. After losing her
baby and being beaten half to death, she changed her life around. She could
have gotten worse and still continue to come after Cameron, but she didn't. She
turned her life around and got her baby back and found love in Kareem and is
now also being a mother to his daughter. Finishing washing my body, I hurried
and jumped out the shower. But as I was getting out, I slipped and fell; landing
hard on the floor. Cameron came running in the bathroom and seeing me on the
floor, he scooped me up bridal style. He ran out, grabbed a pair of sweats and a
t-shirt, and helped me into my clothes. I began to feel sharp pains in my
stomach. I prayed that my baby would be alright. Cameron carried me to the car
and helped me in then placed my seatbelt on. He jogged over to the driver's side
and jumped in and sped to the hospital. By this time, I felt like I was in labor
and it was hurting like hell. I just kept praying that nothing happened to my
baby and that they could stop the pain I was in. Cameron pulled up to Research
Medical Center in five minutes and pulled right up to the entrance and ran in the
hospital to get help. He came back out with a wheelchair and a few nurses. This
nigga lifted me up out the car after taking my seatbelt off. He placed me and the
wheelchair and the nurses did the rest.

"Hey, sweetie. What's your name?" one of the nurses asked me.

"Sidney Hill," I replied.

"OK, Sidney. How far along are you?" the nurse asked again.

"I'm almost 6 months. It's too soon for me to have my baby. Please do
something," I cried.

"It's ok sweetie. We are going to take you upstairs and they will help you
any way they can," the nurse replied, trying to calm me.

The nurse started to roll the wheelchair towards the elevator, and we got in
and headed up to labor and delivery. We arrived and they rushed me to a room
and started checking me in where I found out I was in labor. The doctor came in
and said she was going to do everything she could to stop it since I was too
early to have the baby. They got the IV started and began to give me fluids and
the medicine to stop labor I think they said it was called Terbutaline or
something like that.

2 hours later…

I was still sitting in this bed where I was still feeling these contractions and
they were hurting like hell. Tears were coming out my eyes and I just knew I

was going to have my baby early and I just was praying that my baby would survive. At five and a half months, I was scared for my baby and it was my fault for ever jumping out the shower as I did. The doctor finally came back in to speak to us.

"Sidney, I'm sorry to tell you this but we have not been able to stop the labor so I will be giving you this medicine called Betamethasone. It is an in-utero steroid for premature babies whose lungs aren't quite yet developed. I'm very sorry about this. We have tried to stop the contractions to no avail. Now, I'm going to be honest with you about the chance of survival which is fifty to seventy percent rate. As of right now, all I can say is say a prayer to the Man upstairs. Now, let me check your cervix and see how far you are dilated," the doctor explained. I nodded my head and laid back as the doctor began. "Ok, so it looks like you are about 4 centimeters dilated," the doctor informed us.

Cameron came over and held my hand and kissed my cheek. We prayed that God would save this baby. The doctor walked out of the room then a nurse came in and administered the medicine. The pain started to get more intense and I screamed out.

"Aghhhh, shit! This shit hurts! Oh my god, baby," I yelled.

"Baby, I'm right here for you. I promise I'm not going anywhere," Cameron reassured me.

I'm glad that he is here with me and he has stuck by my side. Next thing I know I felt a gush of fluid come from between my legs.

"Cameron, go get somebody. I think my water just broke," I screamed.

He ran into action and grabbed a nurse in no time. Cameron ran back in the room with a nurse on his heels.

"What's going on, Mrs. Hill?" the nurse asked.

"Ughhh, I think my water broke. I need something for the pain," I screamed out.

"Let me check and see and then we will go from there Mrs. Hill," the nurse informed us. The nurse checked me. "Umm, looks like your water did break. Now, Imma go get something for the pain and send the doctor in," the nurse informed us.

She walked out and then a few minutes later, she came back in with the doctor and a pain medicine she administered through the IV.

"Sidney, I hear that your water broke so let me go ahead and check your cervix again," the doctor stated. She checked my cervix. "You are about 6 centimeters dilated. I want to inform you that now that your water broke it should move along real quick now," the doctor stated.

"Thank you, doctor," Cameron replied.

The doctor turned and walked out, and Cameron picked up his phone and started calling and texting everyone since we were having this baby tonight.

"Cameron, baby. I wanna apologize. I shouldn't have jumped out the shower like I did, or we wouldn't be here right now," I cried.

"Now baby, this is nobody's fault. Who's to say that you wouldn't have gone into to labor all on your own? We don't know what could have happened if you didn't fall," Cameron confessed.

I nodded my head and he sat back down next to me and began to finish calling and texting everyone. I started screaming out in pain again. These contractions were beginning to become more and more frequent. I'm scared that things will not go the way that I wanted them to go. I really wanted this baby no matter who the father is. The pain was beginning to become unbearable.

"Argggghhhh, shit! This shit fucking hurts!" I screamed.

Cameron ran over to me and began to hold my hand as I fought through the pain. There was a knock on the door and in walked the doctor.

"Hey, it's time to check your cervix again, Ms. Hill," the doctor informed me.

I didn't even reply. I was ready for this shit to be over with already. If my baby survived this then I was going to count my blessings for damn sure. The doctor began to check my cervix as I laid back and tried to relax.

"Ok, Hun, it looks like you are about 7 centimeters dilated. It's almost time for this little one to make its grand entrance," the doctor stated.

"Thank you, doc," Cameron replied.

I was still in shock and in pain, things were moving around pretty fast. Most people say that you will be in labor for hours or maybe even days, but I haven't even been here long, and mines was moving real fucking fast. I just hope that wasn't a bad sign though. I decided I was going to pray that God made sure my baby was ok when he or she arrived. Bowing my head, I said a quick prayer. Looking up, the doctor and Cameron were staring at me strangely.

"Why are y'all staring at me like that?" I asked both of them.

"Baby, I just want you to know, I love you no matter what happens today," Cameron said being all weird.

"Umm, Cam. I love you, too but why are you being weird? I know you love me," I replied.

"Ok, Ms. Hill. I don't have an easy way to tell you this, but your labor is moving along really fast and I say you should be ready to push within an hour to two maybe even less. Listen, I'mma be real honest with you. I'm not going to sugarcoat anything so please don't take this the wrong way," I nodded, and she continued. "You are really early going in to labor so with that survive miracles happen every day. I'm hoping today will be one of those miracles. If he or she does she will have a long road to go until she is able to come home. Now, I know that's not what you are hoping will happen, but I just wanted to be honest with you guys," the doctor stated in a matter of fact tone.

"Thank you, doctor, for being honest and not giving us false hope," I cried.

2 hours later…

The doctor knocked and came in to check to see if it was time to start pushing. I hope it was time because I was ready. I had this strong urge to push and the doctor had been ignoring me for the past hour.

"Ok, let's check you out and see what you are dilated to. It looks like you are ready to push Hun. Let me go get the team so we can begin delivering this bundle of joy," the doctor exclaimed.

When I looked up there were a few extra people in the room. They all were moving around the room very quickly preparing for my delivery. The doctor put on some scrub like gown over her clothes I guess for delivery shit I don't know I ain't never been through no shit like this before. Cameron came over to me and he looked nervous and scared all at once. He kissed me on my forehead while holding my hand.

"Ok, Sidney. On your next contraction I want you bare down and push for me ok," the doc requested.

Soon as I nodded my head, a contraction hit me outta nowhere. I swear even in the movies after the doc says to push on your next contraction, that's when the next one hits it never fails. I grabbed Cameron's hand and bore down and began to start pushing. That shit was hurting like hell with no pain meds.

"Aghhhh, fuck! This shit hurts," I screamed.

"Ok, relax and breathe Hun. I can see the head," the doctor informed us.

I laid back and was using the breathing techniques I saw them use in the movies. Cameron was standing there calm as hell, so I looked over at him. He was looking even more scared than before, but I don't have time to worry about that right now. I have to stay focused on bringing my baby in this world. I know I know that sounds fucked up, but I can't focus on anything other than this baby right now.

"Ok, Sidney, get ready and start pushing again sweetie," the doctor stated.

I grabbed Cameron's hand and began to start pushing as soon as the contractions started. I was screaming out in pain trying to push this baby out.

Next thing I know, I felt the baby sliding out and Cameron hit the floor. One of the nurses rushed to him trying to get him to wake up, but I guess it wasn't working. He really fainted when the baby slide out. I just shook my head. The doctor cut the cord and handed the baby off to the nurses. The baby was so tiny I began to cry for my baby. The nurse rushed the baby over to the incubator. Tears just slid down my face as I watch the nurses' work on my daughter. I knew she was gone before the nurses even looked over at me; she never had a chance to even live her life.

"Sidney, sweetie. I'm so sorry for your loss. I will have them clean the baby up and let you have some alone time with your daughter. Again, I'm so sorry about your loss. Is there anyone in the waiting room that you would like to be sent back here with you guys as well?" the doctor apologized.

I nodded my head and informed her that our family was out there. She finished cleaning me up then turned and walked out the room. About ten minutes later, the nurse walked over with my baby girl wrapped up in the receiving blanket and a pink hat on her head. The tears began to fall down uncontrollably. Soon as the nurse placed the baby in my arms in walked both of our parents. My mother and Cameron's mom ran over to me.

"Aww, baby. I'm so sorry. The doctor told us what happened. I see my son-in-law passed out huh," my mom said.

I nodded my head as I continued to look down at my baby girl. I couldn't take my eyes off her thinking just maybe by me holding her she will start breathing on her own at least. They say a mother's love is everything and could even bring a baby back. I started to take the blanket off her just to look at her fingers and toes. I have to look at every part of my child. As I sat there expecting her body, I noticed her chest begin to rise and fall. I pushed the call light. I couldn't believe this; my baby was breathing. There was a knock on the door and in walked one of the nurses.

"How may I help you, Ms. Hill?" The nurse asked.

"I think she is starting to breathe on her own. Look, her chest is rising and falling," I informed the nurse.

She looked down with a sad look on her face the looked back up at me with the same sad look like I was imagining my baby breathing or something, but I know I wasn't. my baby was breathing, and I knew she was.

"Umm, Ms. Hill? She's not breathing. She isn't moving but I can check to see if I can feel a pulse for you," the nurse said solemnly.

"You can check her pulse all you want. She is breathing. I know what the hell I saw," I yelled.

The nurse checked the baby's pulse. She looked up and shook her head. I know I didn't imagine her chest rising and falling. I just started crying again. Tears were falling down my face and then I looked up to see Cameron was finally up. He was looking at me and seeing the tears in my eyes, he jumped up and rushed over to me.

"Baby, what's wrong? Why are you crying?" Cameron exclaimed.

"The baby is a girl and she didn't make it. She wasn't breathing when she was born. It's all my fault that she is dead. If I wouldn't have jumped out the shower like I did and fallen then she wouldn't have been born today," I cried.

"Look, Sidney. We talked about this earlier, baby. It's not your fault. Who's to say that even if you didn't fall getting out the shower you would have had her early? It's no way of knowing what would have happened. God never makes mistakes. Everything happens for a reason. Though I don't know what that reason is for taking our little girl, we have to take this as it is right now. We will get through this. We need to give her a name though, mama," Cameron stated, trying to comfort me.

I know he was trying to make me feel better, but I just couldn't believe what he was saying right now. I wanted my baby and I just couldn't be ok with the fact that I had to let her go and go home without her. I handed Cameron the baby so he could hold her for his self and see how I was feeling at this very moment. As he took the baby out my arms, tears slid down his face just like they were on mine. I was in my own thoughts while Cameron and everyone else in the room was spending their last minutes with the baby. But just like Cameron said, we have to give this little one a name and I was leaning towards Diane Michelle Hill.

"I know you guys think I'm crazy about how I been acting but it's hard to accept that my baby girl will never get a chance at life. I really wanted this baby even if she was the product of rape, but I was going to love her anyway because it wasn't her fault on how she got here. With that being said I have come up with a name for her. I hope you all agree with it," I concluded.

"Sidney, look sweetheart, we won't hold anything against you. We all are here for you no matter what. We don't look at you any different. This loss is hard on all of us and I really do understand I've been there before with losing a child. Remember you were a twin baby. Now, tell us my grandchild's name," my mom commented.

"Her name will be Diane Michelle Hill," I disclosed.

Everyone nodded their heads in agreement with the name. We all sat around spending our last moments with the baby before I called the nurse in so she could take her. This loss was going to be a hard one since I actually got to hold my baby this time around. I lay back in bed just staring up at the ceiling asking God to show me a sign that things will be a lot better and I will be able to have the child that I desperately wanted to have. As I was staring up, I must have dozed off.

Chapter 12

Patience

J couldn't believe tomorrow was the day that we were gonna lay Sidney's baby girl to rest. I was still shocked because I know how she feels but I've never had to deliver a baby early and they come out not breathing. Cameron said he passed out when she pushed the baby out. I laughed when he told us that. But on a serious note, I was hurting for them. Cameron came over the other day and told us Sidney wouldn't get out the bed or even eat. All she did was cry and stay in bed. So, Kareem and I helped Cameron plan the funeral for the baby since Sidney couldn't. I just wanted to help her out any way that I could. That's why I'm over their house now as we speak trying to get her to come to the door. Cameron was out getting last minute things together for tomorrow morning. I was standing there at the door bamming and Sidney still didn't come to open it; even after banging for a good thirty minutes. So, I picked up my phone out my purse and called Cameron.

"Hello, Patience. What's up? I'm kinda busy getting things set up and viewing the baby's body before tomorrow," Cameron elaborated.
"Well, Cam. I'm at your house and I've been bamming for the last thirty minutes to no avail of getting Sidney to come to the door," I mentioned.

"Fuck! Here I come man. Aye, I will be right back then we can view the body. I got an emergency with my wife," he sounded worried as he replied. We hung up the phone and I went back to my car to have a seat until he got to the house.

One hour later…

Cameron finally pulled up and he jumped out the car and headed to the door. I followed behind him as he walked around the house calling Sidney's name with no answer. I was starting to get a bad feeling about this. Finally, we walked up to their room and there was no Sidney in the bed. Cameron walked to their bathroom that was in their room and tried to open the door but it was locked so he started bamming trying to get her to open. I had a feeling something wasn't right here.

"Cameron, I think you should break the door down. Hurry up please. I don't like this feeling I have in my gut that something is wrong," I confessed.

He started kicking the door and it flew open finally and what we say was not a sight to see. Inside the bathtub sat Sidney in a tub full of water with her wrist slit. I ran over to her and checked for a pulse. It was faint but she still had one. Cameron was crying and everything screaming "No!" and asking why would she do this to them.

"Cameron, I need you to pull yourself together! We need to get her to the hospital now!" I bellowed.

Cameron jumped up in action. He grabbed something to wrap around her wrist and then he grabbed a robe and pulled her out the water. Cam put it on her then ran to his car as I ran behind him. He placed her in the back seat and I climbed in the back with her while he drove as fast as he could towards Research Medical. A thirty-minute drive turned into a five-minute one. Cameron parked in the emergency entrance not caring where as he hopped out the car and came around to get Sidney out then ran inside the hospital. I got out of the car and went to park his car for him. Then walked inside the hospital, I looked around and saw Cameron sitting in a chair in the waiting room with tears in his eyes. I knew he was going through it right now; this is his wife. I walked over and sat beside him. I didn't say a thing. I just sat there cause when Cameron is ready he will talk. I picked up my phone to send Kareem a text to let him know where we were and what happened.

Me: *Hey babe. I'm at the hospital with Cameron. Sidney tried to kill herself.*

Kareem: *I'm omw now. I'mma drop the kids off with my parents and then I'm there.*

I looked over at Cameron and he was sending out messages I guess to their family. Sidney losing her daughter took a toll on her and I know that's what caused her to think that she needed to take her life. I had the same thoughts while in the hospital after Sean caused me to lose my baby but I had to think about my living daughter that needed me.

"Cameron, Kareem said he is on his way after he drops the girls off," I stated.

"Ok, thanks for being here with me Patience. You don't have to stay. Our parents are on the way to sit up here with me," Cameron replied.

"Cameron, I am staying to find out what they say. Sidney has become a really good friend of mine. So, I'm just gonna sit here," I argued.

"Ok, Ma. That's fine with me. I also want to let you know that I am proud of you and so is Sidney. We spent many nights up late talking about how much of a change you have made. You've got your daughter back, you're getting married, and you have gained another daughter. That deserves some praise no doubt," Cameron acknowledged.

"Thank you, Cameron. That means a lot to me, especially how I tried to ruin your relationship and how I lied to you when I was pregnant with Alyssa," I added.

Before we could continue with our conversation, their parents walked in followed by Kareem. I just sat there in my thoughts. Just thinking about everything I put them through and everything that Sidney has been through because of Sean. That poor woman has had it very hard. I sat there and prayed that everything would be alright. Kareem walked up, pulled me up out my seat and hugged me tight. I welcomed this comfort.

"Cameron, how you holding up?" Kareem asked.

"I'm hanging in there best I can," Cameron replied.

I sat down and Kareem sat next to me while their parents came over and took a seat as well. This was the wrong time to be thinking this but I was sitting here thinking that Cameron's team made the AFC championship. They were going against the Patriots this weekend and Cameron's head wasn't gonna be in the game like it should. *Two hours later…*

We were still sitting around waiting for a doctor to come out. Cameron was up pacing the waiting room. Finally, a doctor walked out.

"The family of Sidney Hill," the doctor called out.

We all stood up and walked over to the doctor but waited for him to speak.

"Hi, I'm doctor Rome. I treated Ms. Hill. She is going to be ok but she will have to be on a 72 hour suicide watch. She's going to the psychiatric part of the hospital as soon as a bed is ready. We will be moving her there so you guys can go see her, but I will warn you now, she is a little out of it and she will be like that until the pain medicine wears off. She will be in pain for a while and I will give her pain meds to go home with. If you need anything, just have them page me. This nurse here, Nurse Cassandra, will show you to Sidney's room," the doctor stated.

"Thank you, doctor. I'm her husband Cameron Hill," Cameron introduced his self, shaking his hand.

"Yes, I know who you are. Star quarterback Cameron Hill that plays for the Outlawz," the doctor beamed.

I just shook my head; here we go with a fan. Cameron smiled and nodded his head. The doctor turned and walked away and Nurse Cassandra walked us all to Sidney's room. We walked in and she was facing the wall; looking like she was sleep. Cameron walked over to her bed and sat beside her.

"Sid, baby. Why would you try and leave me like that, Ma?" Cameron cried.

She didn't even open her eyes to say anything to him as he sat there And talked to her.

Chapter 13

Sidney

I was laying here listening to Cameron cry to me about what would he be like if I left him here by his self, but he just doesn't understand how I'm feeling right now. I lost my baby and had to push her out dead. That shit hurts like hell. I know that he lost the baby too but for me, it's worse and different. If that makes sense to you. Laying here listening to everybody talk, I finally decided to open my eyes after everyone left out the room. But when I looked around, Cameron was still standing there by the door like he knew I was faking while they were here.

"I knew yo' ass was faking but check it, I'm going to be here every step of the way. I need you to get better. I know it's different for you and I understand that but I need you to get better, Ma. Real shit I need you, baby. When you are ready, we will try and have another baby. When you are ready," Cameron confessed with tears in his eyes.

"I'm sorry Cameron. I really am. It just hurts hella hard for me right now. Like I really pushed my dead daughter out of me, and it is killing me inside. Yes, I know I was being selfish but baby, I'm hurting like hell, and just needed an escape. That was the closest thing that I came up with," I cried.

"Look, babe. It's going to be ok. You are going to need to get you some help because I won't be able to live with myself knowing that you tried to take yo' own life over the loss of our child. They will be holding you for 72 hours, but I will be here every step of the way. After your 72 hours, I want you to continue to get the help you need please," Cameron stressed.

I nodded my head understanding and agreeing to what he said. Cameron walked over to me and kissed my lips and I returned the kiss. I can't believe I was so fucking selfish and was going to kill myself. I need to make things right for Cameron and that means me getting better and going back to how we were before the loss of the baby. If that means me getting treatment, then I was all for it.

"Cameron, I'm going to do everything I can to get better and get back to the person I used to be before we loss the baby," I cried harder then I was already crying.

"Well, you get you some rest and I'm going to go home to clean up and rest. I have a game tomorrow. You know we made it to the playoffs, so I got to get this win. I wanna make it to the Super Bowl this year. If you need me, call me. I will be back in the morning to see you before my game," Cameron stated.

He kissed my forehead then turned and walked out. As I was sitting there in my own thoughts, I realized that I have to do better. I can't leave Cameron here to mourn me and our baby on his own. He needed me now more than ever. As I was sitting here in my thoughts there was a knock on the door.

Knock...Knock...

Patience walked in with this sad look on her face. I knew she was feeling sorry for me, but I didn't want her to at all. I just want to be happy again and I know if people are taking petty on me and everything, it's going to be hard for me to get over this.

"Patience, please don't feel sorry for me, Hun. That's just going make me feel sad and I don't want to be sad anymore. This has woken me up so I'm gonna need you to just be there for me and that's it. Now, I need you to do me a favor," I admitted.

"Anything you need I'm here," Patience answered.

"Ok, look. I need you to look after both shops for me until I am well enough to come back to work. Let the girls know that you will be in charge until I come back, please. I know I'm putting a lot on you right now but since you are going to be working in my other shop you might as well be the manager of the new one. You can start by helping out in my other shop until the new one is ready for the grand opening in a few weeks," I offered.

"Oh my God, is you serious right now? You really want me to be the manager of the new shop? But I will help with both though for sure while you are down but look, you will get through this. You have an amazing man that loves you and will be there every step of the way," Patience exclaimed.

"Thank you, Patience. And yea, I know Cameron is so amazing and I love him. I am going to get it together. I need to get back to the old me before the loss of my baby," I cried.

"Well, you get some rest and I will be back to see you soon to give you an update," Patience replied.

She bent down and gave me a hug then turned and walked out of the room. I laid back and got comfortable while closing my eyes to get some rest. As I lay there, I thought about all the things I've been through since meeting Sean. He has dragged me through hell and back and I can finally move on with my life. Now that he is gone and never coming back, I just hope that the police don't come back around but you never know with KCPD. It's been times where people have been missing for months or even years and still haven't been found so who knows. We will see what happens. I drifted off to sleep for a while.

Looking around, I didn't know where I was at. It looked like a playground of some sort. I saw a lil girl playing on the swing set, so I walked over to her and kneeled down to look at her. She looked identical to the daughter I just loss. She looked up at me and waved then smiled.

"Hi mommy. It's me, Diane Michelle Hill," the lil girl said, introducing herself.

"Oh my God, baby! How are you doing? Are they taking care of you? Mommy misses you so much," I cried.

"Mommy, I'm fine. Really, I am. I came to you to talk to you. Look, I know you are hurting but I want you to move on and enjoy your life. Give my little brother and sister the life that they deserve. I don't blame you at all. I want you to be happy with Pops. He needs you right now and you need him as well," she confessed.

I nodded my head and knew that I needed to get myself together and do right by Diane. Cameron needs me now more than ever and I had to be what he needed right now.

"I got you baby girl. I'm going to do better. Now, can I push you on the swing for a little while?" I asked.

"I would love that, but I have to get back," she informed me.

I looked at her with a sad look and she smiled and ran up to me to give me a hug while kissing my cheek. She then ran off.

The next morning…

It was the next morning and I was waking up, so I sat up in the bed and the nurse walked in to check on me. There was a knock on the door and Cameron and the doctor walked in.

"Hey baby. How are you feeling this morning?" Cameron asked.

"I'm actually feeling a little better today. After the night I had, I have a new outlook on life," I confessed.

"Well, good morning, Ms. Hill. I am Dr. Rome. I treated you last night when you were brought in. They will be transporting you to the building next door for 72 hours. Are you in agreeance that you need the help we are going to provide you?" Dr. Rome asked.

I nodded my head that I agree. The doctor continued to talk to me about my care as long as I was here. Looking over at Cameron, he looked so handsome. I hope wherever they move me to they had a TV where I could watch the game he was playing in today. My baby was playing the New England Patriots in the playoffs for the AFC Championship. This is the first time in years that they could make it all the way to the Super Bowl in a long ass time. I am proud of him and I'm glad that my plan to kill myself backfired or I wouldn't be here to see this moment for him.

"Umm, Dr. Rome. After this inpatient treatment, I would like to keep going with outpatient care," I confessed.

"Ok, great. We can set that up before you leave here," Dr. Rome replied.

Cameron looked at me and smiled. He must be proud of me. The doctor turned around and walked out of the room. As I was looking into his eyes, Cameron was looking into mine and I could see the passion there. I knew this man is in love with me by the look in his eyes.

"Cameron, baby. I love you and I'm sorry about yesterday. I want you to put all that behind you today and whoop them Patriots ass. I will be watching on the TV since I can't be there to watch in person," I stated.

Cameron smiled then walked over to me and gave me a kiss it wasn't just any kiss either he was so passionate about it showing me his love. We were so into the kiss that we didn't hear the knock on the door until whoever it was cleared their throat.

"Umm-hmm! Sorry to interrupt but we are here to take you to the other building. If you would please have a seat in the wheelchair we can head on over," the nurse announced.

She walked over pushing the wheelchair and Cameron helped me up and over to it. Then we walked out of the room and over to the next building where I will be getting the help I need before I can go home. I was ready to get this over and start my new life with my husband. After seeing my baby girl in my dreams last night, I still didn't have a chance to tell Cameron about it, but I will soon as I get a chance to. We arrived at the other building and she pushed me to the room I was going to be staying in and turned to walk out.

"Ok, this is where you will be till it's time to go home. There will be a nurse to come in and you sign all the paperwork and do your intake and then we will go from there," the nurse advised me.

"Ok, thank you very much," I replied.

She walked out of the room and I looked over at Cameron sitting in the chair next to the bed. I got up out the wheelchair and Cameron jumped up and to help me in the bed. I laid back thinking I must have this private room because of Cameron. I even had a TV in my room. I didn't think they would have one. Cameron must have been the one to have them set this room up like this.

"Cameron, you had them do all this didn't you," I asked?

"Well, yea I did. My wife deserves the best. Plus, I know you can't be there with me today and you want to watch the game. You need this and I will be here every step of the way. Now, I have to get out of here and head to the stadium and get ready for the game," Cameron acknowledged.

He bent down and kissed me then turned and walked out. I laid back and relaxed and waited on a nurse to come in to do my intake. As I was laying there waiting, I drifted off to sleep. These pain meds they have me on got me all drowsy.

Knock...Knock...

A nurse walked in, so I sat up in the bed on turned the TV on but put it on mute. The nurse sat down in the chair by the bed. I looked up at the screen for a second to see the game was just getting ready to start. I hope that this nurse didn't take long.

"Hi, how are you doing Ms. Hill. I'm Nurse Becca. I will be doing your intake so let's get started. So, I see here you are on a 72-hour hold for trying to commit suicide. May I ask what brought you to the point where you wanted to kill yourself?" Nurse Becca asked.

"Well, just about a week ago, I gave birth to a lil girl, but she was stillborn. I felt less of a woman that I couldn't give my husband one thing we were hoping for," I confessed.

"Ok well, sweetheart, your baby dying had nothing to do with you being less of a woman. You will have your day to enjoy your bundle of joy soon. God will give it to you when he knows you are ready and in the great position for what is to come. Now, I don't know what happened or how your life is but things will get better. You will be here for 72 hours and I will be the nurse to care for you and we will get you through this. You will have the baby you and your husband dream of," Nurse Becca replied.

"Thank you. I think I needed to hear that," I stated.

"Ok, next question. Do you feel like you would benefit from this inpatient treatment?" the nurse asked.

"Yes, I think I will. I need this to get better and be the wife and mother I need to be in the future," I informed the nurse.

"Ok, a few more questions and then we will be done. Do you drink alcohol or do any recreational drugs whatsoever?" Nurse Becca asked.

"No drugs and I would have a glass of wine occasionally. Not on an everyday basis," I answered.

"Ok, it says that everything for your stay here is taking care of. I have your address and everything else in your file. That is all I need to know. I already can tell by the bandages on your wrist that you tried to slit your wrist," Nurse Becca stated.

I nodded and looked up at the TV to see my baby running for a touchdown. He got it and I screamed out in excitement.

"Yesssss! Go baby! Touchdown!" I yelled.

"Oh, you a football fan I see," the nurse exclaimed.

"Oh, Nurse Becca, yes I am. My husband is the star quarterback for the Kansas city Outlawz," I informed her.

"The Cameron Hill is your husband? I knew I heard he was off the market finally, but you snagged you a good one honey. I hope they win today so they can make it to the Super Bowl," the nurse stated.

I nodded my head. She got up to hug me and turned and walked out of the room. I laid there and finished watching the game till there was another knock on the door. A nurse walked in with a plate of food for me. She sat it on the table and turned and walked back out the door. I sat there watching the game while eating. This food was actually good.

95

Lovely Ann

You would think that considering its part of the hospital it would be
nasty like the hospital food, but it wasn't it was actually a decent
meal. Finishing up my, I pushed the tray next to the bed so when they
came and got it they could just grab it.
I sat there watching this game and Cameron and his team was winning;
7-28, 3rd quarter with 2 minutes left. They were 3rd and goal. I
was screaming at the TV cause Cameron had the ball and he was
getting ready to throw it, but nobody was open. Next thing you
know, Cameron took off running towards the end zone.
Then, TOUCHDOWN baby! My baby made a touchdown. I
started screaming from excitement. While I was screaming, a nurse ran
in.
"Ms. Hill, are you alright? We heard you screaming at the desk," the
nurse exclaimed.
"Oh my God, yes! I'm fine. I'm just watching my husband's game. I'm
sorry for being so loud," I stated.
"Oh, it's fine, baby. Just try to keep it down out of respect for the
other patients please," the nurse replied.
I nodded my head understanding what she was saying. She turned
and walked out of the room and I finished watching the game. We ended
up winning the AFC Championship. I was proud of my baby and their
team. They finally are going back to the Super Bowl after all these years
of not getting this far. When I got out of here, we were going to
celebrate just how we should; party and all.

Chapter 14

Cameron

J was so excited I couldn't help the smile on my face right now. We won the AFC Championship last week, my wife was home now after being gone for a week, Friday my wife was throwing me a party for a celebration for winning the championship, and today, we were finally getting ready to lay Diane to rest. I know this will be hard for Sidney, but I was going to be here every step of the way. Since she has been home things have been a lot better. Maybe her seeing someone and being in that mental hospital actually was what she needed. After all these years of hurt and pain. All that hurt, and pain, and then the loss of our baby just pushed her over the edge, and she didn't think before she decided to try and kill herself. She didn't even talk to me about how she was feeling. But I'm just glad it didn't end how she wanted to at the time.

I walked in the house and Sidney was just sitting there putting her shoes on. I just came from the funeral home to view the body. Sidney couldn't even make it up there. She wanted to wait for the funeral, and I understood where she was coming from. If I didn't have to finalize the funeral arrangements, I wouldn't have gone either. I kissed Sidney on the forehead and headed up the stairs to go get ready. Walking in the room, Sidney had my suit laid out. I grabbed my towel and walked into the bathroom. Turning the water onto the temperature of my liking, I hopped in the shower and began to let the water run over my body. I was drained after these last few days running around here like a chicken with its head cut off. But I had to get this stuff done for the funeral. The water running down my body was feeling nice and relaxing, but I needed a release and I needed it bad. So, I did what I've been doing the last week now. Don't get me wrong, I'm not complaining. I'm willing to wait as long as possible for my wife to be ready to have sex again and maybe just maybe she will be ready to try and have a baby again. I know it maybe be fast to some of y'all but I'm ready to start a family with my wife. I've wanted this for so long and now that I've finally settled down, I was ready for a family. Who would have thought that me, Cameron Hill, would be married and wanting kids?

I began to grab my dick and jack off in the shower as I started thinking of Sidney's nice as lips wrapped around my pole and it made me rock up even harder. Speeding up I felt my release right there at the tip and just as I was getting ready to cum, I was interrupted by Sidney stopping me. "Naw, let me help you get your release baby," Sidney sexily stated. Shit, she ain't said nothing but a word. I stepped out the shower and I stripped her out of her clothes in no time. Picking her up in the air, I leaned against the bathroom wall and began to eat her pussy just like she liked it. She was cumming in no time. Pulling her down I eased her down onto my pole and began to move in and out of her honeypot, nice and slow just how she likes it. I began to walk into the bedroom while delivering her these slow deep strokes into that slippery wet pussy. I laid her down on the bed and began to kiss on her neck on down to her nipples while still delivering this dick to her middle. Sidney was moaning out like crazy her pussy muscles were tightening up around my pole and she was squeezing the shit out of my dick like she had that mothafucka in a choke hold and I was loving it. I was minutes away from cumming and I know this was going to be a quick one but shit, we didn't have much time anyway. Plus, I haven't had any of this wet pussy in a while anyway.

"Baby, if you want me to pull out you gonna have to release my dick so I don't cum all up in this wet, wet," I moaned out breathlessly.

"Mmmhhhh, shit! I don't care Cameron. Cum all in this pussy baby," Sidney moaned.

Shit, she didn't have to tell me twice. I began to pound into her middle and within minutes I was coating her walls with my seeds. I know that

she maybe end up pregnant but shit she told me to cum in that pussy.
Rolling over after that nice release, I had to get my breathing in order
before I got up and washed up and got dressed. Soon as we got our
breathing was back to normal, I hopped up and pulled Sidney up. We
walked back into the bathroom where we hopped in the shower. I
grabbed her sponge and began to wash her up and then washed myself
up and rinsed off and we both got out and got dressed and then we
were headed out the door. The limo and our family were standing
outside waiting on us to come out. I'm glad everyone showed up on
time today like I requested. Even my teammates were here waiting to
head out. The girls from the shop were here and everything. I looked over
at Sidney and she had tears in her eyes. I hope this was tears of happiness
but I couldn't be so sure just yet.

"Baby, did you do all this for me?" Sidney asked

"I did this for us baby," I replied.

She turned to me and reached up and kissed my lips, but I took it a
step further and deepen the kiss till we were rudely interrupted by my mom.

"Boy, if you don't wait til after this baby's home going to get you some
pussy. She ain't going no damn where. Shit, nigga got a hard-on just from a
damn kiss," mom shouted.

Everyone started laughing at mom and I just shook my head because she had
no filter whatsoever. I just walked past everyone and walked to the limo and the
driver opened the door and the family and Sidney and I got in. We were headed
to the church finally to get this over with. I know it's gonna be a lot of tears
today and I just wanted this day to be over with so we can get back to being
happy and living our best life. I was sitting next to Sidney and she was staring
off into space I knew she had a lot on her mind today but when she was ready to
talk, I am going to be here for her. We pulled up to the church in no time, the
driver opened the door and we all got out the limo. We all walked into the
church and they had us line up and walk in to view the body. As we walked
closer to the pink casket, the tears dropped from my eyes seeing my baby girl
laying there. Sidney gripped my hand tighter as we looked at our baby. She was
tearing up as well.

"I can't do this. It's hard to see her like this. She is our baby. We shouldn't be
burying our daughter at all," Sidney cried.

"I know baby, but we will get through this together. I promise you that ma,"
I stated matter of factly.

We walked to our seats and sat down as everyone else viewed babygirl's body. Everyone was walking up to us hugging us and letting us know they were sorry for our loss. It was kind of overwhelming. Me and Sidney walked up to view the body one last time before they closed her casket. Before we walked back to our seat Sidney leaned down and kissed the baby one last time before they closed the casket.

"I'mma miss you, baby. Mama loves you and will never forget you," Sidney cried.

We walked back to our seats and soon as we took our seats the pastor was up speaking. I must have zoned out because I didn't hear anything the preacher man was saying until Sidney nudged me, and it was my time to get up and say a few words about my baby girl. Getting up I walked to the podium.

"Thank you all for coming today to celebrate our baby girl Diane. I never got to spend time with her but when my wife was pregnant with her. I was there through everything; when she found out she was pregnant and through the DNA test. Some may not know that part, but you know now. I was there when she was going into labor, pushing her out. I passed out when she slipped out ha ha ha. I didn't expect it to be like that. By the time I came to she was already gone so I missed everything after she slipped out. I loved this lil girl from the time that I found out my wife was pregnant with her. I'mma miss you baby girl and we going to remember you till the end of time," I cried.

I walked back to my seat so the next person could come up to speak. I sat there and listened as everyone said something about my baby girl. Then there was this lady I never saw before, and Sidney tensed up so she must have known who she was.

"Sid, baby. Do you know who that lady is?" I asked.

"That's Sean's wife," Sidney replied.

"Now, I don't know this little baby but I'm glad she is dead. My husband will not have no other kids that's not mine," Sean's wife yelled.

Next thing I knew, Sidney, Patience, my mom, and sister and all our family was up out their seats going after her. She tried to run but Sidney grabbed her by the hair and started beating her ass. I jumped up and everyone else did as well to grab their significant other. They all were beating that girl so bad it was blood everywhere. One of the men helped this lady up and dragged her out of the church. I couldn't believe this bitch got up there and said some shit like that. I knew this was going

100

to cause some shit somehow some kinda way. It was only a matter of time before the shit was going to hit the fan.

"Look everyone. Sit down so we can finish the service. Don't let that ratchet ruin the celebration we are having for Diane today," I announced.

Everyone went and took their seats and the pastor finished up the service. As soon as the service was over the pallbearers got up to take the casket to the hearse and after they walked the casket out, we got up and walked behind them to watch as they placed baby girl into the hearse. Sidney stood there and cried as she watched them placed the baby inside. After the baby was placed inside, we walked to the limo where we all got in and then we headed to the burial site where Diane will be buried. As I was sitting here thinking about everything that happened today, I was just in complete and utter shock that this man's wife came in the church and acting as she did. Breaking free from my thoughts I noticed that we arrived at the burial site. We all got out and walked to the tent and had a seat in the chairs that was in front of where her casket was sitting.

"We have gathered to mourn the passing and to celebrate the life of Diane Hill. We have come together to grieve and to give thanks for her life. For the next brief space in time, we will cry and laugh almost simultaneously. As human beings, we are only creatures gifted to feel such a range of emotions all at the same time. It is good that we can do it together.

Whenever a death occurs, those of us who remain behind enter a space in time that is quite out of the ordinary. Whether we recognize this or not, this is sacred time—a time that holds potential for healing and insight and understanding that does not come readily in ordinary time. With the death of someone we have known and loved, something in each one of us dies too. We are reminded of the frailties and the gifts of our relationships. We become more aware that we live in fragile human bodies. We may come to know a heightened consciousness of what is precious and what is true. Indeed, with the passing of a loved one, we encounter our own mortality.

When we gather in the Christian community, this sacred time is heightened by our affirmation that there is eternal life after death- and it is here, together, where we glimpse the mystery of the mansion with many rooms that Jesus promised his disciples as he prepared to leave them. There is nothing we can touch, nothing we can describe or pin down—nothing concrete—but the mystery of death has the power to bring

us to the threshold of faith. In this extraordinary and sacred time, what
we encounter is the power of grief—and the power of hope. It is
here, together, where we may intuit the meaning of Paul's words when
he affirms that "Neither life nor death……. Can separate us from the love
of God." So, I welcome you to this time out of ordinary time. I invite you
to pause, to let it settle in that a precious life has passed from among us.
We can use the gift of our worship and our memories to bring comfort
and peace and joy and laughter to one another as we remember Diane

and… perhaps… we will enjoy a trace of Diane's presence as we
share together.
God of birth and life and death and beyond, on this day the blessings
of earth. On this day the blessings of sea and sky. To open us to life
to ground us in life to fill us with life and with wonder. On those, we
love this day and on every human family the blessings of heaven,
the blessings of earth the blessing of sky and sea. In the rising of the sun
and its setting, in the whiteness of the moon and its seasons, in the
infinity of space and its shining stars, you are
God and we bless you. May we know the harmony of heaven in
the relationships of earth, and may we know the expanse of its
mystery within us. We take your promised peace with us. Amen,"
The preacher prayed.
We all watched as the baby's casket was being lowered into the
ground. Afterwards, we all walked back to the limo. We were headed back
to the crib for the repast. Pulling off towards the crib, we all chatted
with one another till we pulled up to the crib. The driver let us out and we
all headed for the door. Sidney unlocked the door and we all walked
inside. Sidney and I headed upstairs I guess she was thinking about what
I was thinking; getting out these damn clothes. Walking into the room,
I went into my closet and grabbed some sweats and one of my DBK
shirts and laid them on the bed. I went into the bathroom and removed
my clothes and washed up a little bit then walked back into the room in
just my boxers and started to get dressed. Sidney was already changed
and was walking out of the room. I finished getting dressed and headed
back down the stairs to everyone else. Looking around, everyone was in
a good mood including Sidney. Everyone was here; Patience and
Kareem was here with their kids. Mom and Pops were here, and they
were getting along and looking like they were in love again. Things

were actually looking up for everyone. Shit, even Lucas and his crew and family were here. Things are looking great now the cops haven't been snooping around anymore only thing we have to worry about right now is Sean's wife but after today she shouldn't be a problem anymore. Just looking around at everyone I was amazed that my life has changed so much that I am now married and living my best life. Never would I have thought that I would be married and wanting a family. But I do and it means everything to me, and Sidney makes me the happiest man alive.

Epilogue

Kareem

Things were going well for me and Patience. I have finally come to terms that my baby mama will not be here to see our daughter grow up and everything. I have taken the necessary steps for Patience to adopt Khalilah. We are planning our wedding and are set to get married in 2 months now. I was also adopting Alyssa since Rick has signed over his rights because his wife doesn't want him involved in his daughter's life.

I walked into the house from a long day at the hospital and when I walked in, I saw Patience and the girls knocked out on the couch. It looked so amazing.

I took my phone out and snapped a picture of them all. This is the life that I have dreamed of for so long.

Patience

I must have fallen asleep putting the girls down for their nap. Opening my eyes, I saw Kareem standing in the living room smiling, looking over at us and it put a smile on my face to see him so happy. Who would have thought I would be so happy with Kareem and that it wouldn't be Cameron that I would be making a life with?

"Kareem, you are looking like a creep standing there just smiling at us," I laughed.

He just laughed at me and came over and gave me a kiss then kissed both the girls. Kareem helped me take them both to their rooms and lay them in their beds. Going back to the front room, we both sat and just talked about how much our life has changed and what the plans were for the next couple of months. Then Kareem got up and walked into the room and came back with an envelope. He handed it to me, and I opened it. Inside the envelope were adoption papers for Khalilah. It brought tears to my eyes. I knew we were talking about it, but I never knew he went and got the paperwork started.

"Kareem, when did you do this? I never knew you went and did this," I cried.

"Well, I've been getting things in order for about a month now. And I am ready for you to be her mother. I have finally come to terms that Khalilah is not going to be here to see Khalilah grow up and I want you to be everything that she will need in a mother if you still want to," he stated.

"Yes, baby. I still want to," I cried.

We kissed and hugged and laid down on the couch where we just talked till, we fell asleep.

Cameron

Things with me and Sidney have been great. She found out a few weeks ago that she was pregnant again and this time, we are having twins. And oh my god was Sidney mean as fuck right now. These babies was taking her through it. But I was happy that we have our babies. Today, we are heading to the doctor to go check on the twins. Since they have her on high risk, we go every two weeks and she is on bed rest till delivery. Patience has been handling the shops for her. Sidney checks in with Patience everyday. As for the playoffs, we won the Super Bowl for the first time in forever and I was proud of my team. We worked together and did it.

Sidney

Here we are once again walking into the doctor's office to check on the twins. Yes, you heard me right. I am pregnant again but this time with twins and I am overjoyed with happiness. I can't wait to meet these two little bundles of joy. Today, we are going to find out what we are having and I am hoping for one of each. Things between us have been great since the funeral some months back. I've been trying to hide the fact that I am pregnant as long as I could but finally, I couldn't hide it anymore and he made me come and get checked out and I'm glad that I did. Patience has been a big help with the shop since I am on complete bed rest till these little ones decide to grace us with their presence. It will be some months from now.

Laying back on the table, I waited for the nurse to come in and start on my ultrasound. Cameron was sitting there on his phone with his mother and pops because they wanted to know what the baby is. But I really wanted everyone to wait til the gender reveal party next week but they just couldn't wait. So, I had them promise that they wouldn't tell anybody at all. There was a knock on the door and in walked the nurse.

"Are you guys ready to see what you are having today?" the nurse asked.

"Yes, we can't wait to see what they are," Cameron exclaimed.

He was too excited as was I. The nurse had me lay back on the bed and raise my shirt and then she squirted the cold gel on my belly while placing the Doppler on my stomach and started moving it around. As soon as she started, the babies started moving. I looked up at the screen and there I saw my babies moving on the screen. Just looking at them brought tears to my eyes.

"Ok, here is baby A. Now, let's see if it will be cooperative and let us see if it is a he or she," the nurse stated.

She began to move around the Doppler again and the baby just kept moving and crossing its legs till finally it gave up seeing how the nurse wasn't giving up either.

"Looks like we have a boy for baby A. Now, let's see if baby B will be a bit more cooperative seeing how baby A is stubborn," the nurse exclaimed.

"I hope so cuz baby boy been giving me hell," I laughed.

"Looks like we have a girl for baby B. Congrats to the both of you," the nurse exclaimed.

I was smiling from ear to ear. I had my son's name picked out already. He was going to be Cameron Hill Jr. Now my daughter, I still was thinking on her name. I wanted something different but unique. After the loss of our first daughter, who would have thought months later I would be here again getting ready to welcome two new babies in this world in just a few short months. God has truly been amazing. There are times where I think of Diane, but I know she is in a better place and will be watching over her brother and sister.

Thank you all for taking this journey with us and letting us tell our story. I hope you all enjoyed it. Who knows, we may come back for another book.

Yayy! Book 4 is finally complete. Thank you for taking this ride with me and sticking it out. Make sure you all read and leave a review. Check out the sneak peek of what's to come next.

Love Me, Or Leave Me But You Can't Have Both

By: Lovely Ann

Chapter 1

Valencia

I've been running back and forth to the doctor for the past 2 years now and I was just so tired of going back and forth. Booker and I have been trying to have a baby for 3 years now and it just wasn't happening. So, she was going to all types of specialist to see what she could do to have a baby at this rate she was just going to give up. she didn't want to have a surrogate she seen those lifetime movies and them bitches just go crazy and end up falling for the man and trying to kill the wife and she just couldn't get down with that shit. So, I'm guessing my other option would be adoption. I give up on trying on my own anymore. As I walked out the office, I hit the locks for my brand new 2018 Telsa and hopped in and was headed to my husband Booker's office to let him know that this was the last time that I go to the doctor to try anything else. We have tried the IUI if you don't know what that is it is Intrauterine insemination and what that means is where the sperm is matched up with my egg inside my uterus. We have tried that a total of 6 times but was unsuccessful it either didn't happen or I had a miscarriage. We also tried the IVF which is the In Vitro Fertilization where they extract the eggs and retrieve a sample of sperm, and then manually combine an egg and the sperm in a lab dish the embryos are then transferred to the uterus. We have done that also a total of 4 or 5 times and I

was just so over it now. Music blasting through my speakers reminded me I
need to get out my thoughts and pay attention.

Can we get a room
    And we ain't gotta tell nobody
    it's just me, and it's just you
    and what we do in here is private
    cut your phone off
    make sure the door is locked
    its midnight gotta leave out by 4 o'clock
    sneaking and freaking it's Friday the weekend
    I'm just getting started I don't wanna leave you

I pulled up to the office in no time and I hopped out and head inside
the office. As I walked in the receptionist gave me this look like I
wasn't supposed to be here but I brushed it off and kept on walking
to Bookers office. Soon as I got to his office, I thought I heard moaning but
I took it as maybe he was watching porn like he always did during the
day so I just walked in what I walked in on I never would have expected
to see Kelli Booker's assistant bent over his desk getting fuck by
my husband. All I saw was red and I ran at full speed and just
started beating on Kelli and Booker at the same time. I couldn't believe
this man, after all, I have done for him giving him 16 years of my life and
3 years of marriage Nah he ain't getting off that easy.
"Really Booker, after all, I've done for you, you turn around and screw
this bitch I just can't believe you right now." I turned to Kelli. "And
you how could you sleep with my husband bitch."
"Gurllll I been fucking your husband for 3 years and we have 2 kids. I
gave him something that you can't give him. Yeah, I know you can't
have kids bitch. And no, I don't feel bad about nothing I've done."
This bitch was really sitting here telling me she fucked my man and had
2 kids by this nigga awl hell Nah. She bout to get her ass beat again. I ran
up on her and just started swinging on her I was getting the best of her
too until someone grabbed me around my waist and pulled me out of
the office. I looked up and it was my husband's brother Carter.
"Get the fuck off me, Carter!!! Booker don't bring your ass back to my
house tonight I want a divorce its fucking over, you treat me like this
and got a whole ass family with this bitch fuck you and her."
"Valencia, we haven't been happy for a long time and I don't love
you anymore I don't know why I let this marriage go on for so long

you can't give me the one thing that I want, and that's children and Kelli here can. So, you being mad I can give 2 fucks about so get the fuck out of my office."

"Fuck you, Booker. I hate you."

For him to speak to me like that was a shock so I just turned and walked out of the office and out the building. As soon as I walked outside, I let the tears fall I couldn't believe this shit I've been down for this man for 16 fucking years and he turns around and does this. I'm taking this nigga for everything he is worth or that he got he is gonna pay for playing me. I may sound bitter, but I don't give a fuck.

Oh, shit, I'm being all rude I'm telling yall my story but I never introduced myself. Well my name is Valencia Ivy and I'm 35 going on 36 I own my own restaurant I'm married to Booker Ivy and have been with him for 16 going on 17 years we have been married for 3 years now and have been trying to have a family but it just wasn't working out in our favor well in my favor anyway as you can see, he already has 2 kids with that bitch, Kelli. As I was driving towards my house, I couldn't stop thinking of our wedding day now we were headed for divorce.

It was April 13, 2015, I was sitting in the dressing room I was putting my wedding dress on getting ready to marry my best friend. My girls were in here trying to make me happy but I was crying because I was scared that he may not love me like I do but they were telling me that he does love me like I do so I was going to go with that. The girls were going to work on my hair and makeup before it was my time to walk down that aisle. As I was sitting there someone knocked on the door and my girl Nora went to the door and cracked it to see who was at the door and it was my pops he walked in and looked around at all of us sitting around talking.

"Ladies can I have a moment alone with my daughter please."

They all got up and walked out as they were leaving, they gave pops a hug.

"What's up pop's?"

"Babygirl I just wanna make sure you are sure this is what you want to do although yall have been together for some time I still don't think he is the man for you right now."

"Dad I really appreciate you I do but I'm sure this is what I want to do don't worry if things go left you taught me well on what to do and to take him for everything he got."

Laughing my dad gave me a hug and walked out the door. I was sitting

there in my own thoughts waiting for my time to come when it was my time to walk out. I place the veil over my face and grabbed my bouquet and got ready to walk out of my dressing room. as I walked out my pops were standing right outside my door and were waiting for me. as if on cue the song I wanted to walk down the aisle to come on.
See first of all
*   I know these so-called playas wouldn't tell you this*
But I'ma be real and say what's on my heart
Let's take this chance and make this love feel relevant
* Didn't you know I loved you from the start, yeah*
As the doors to the church opened everyone turned and looked at me and my father as we began to walk down the aisle. I was looking at Booker dressed in an all-white suit and my eyes just began to tear up and the waterworks began, and I couldn't control it if I wanted to. A few more steps and I was standing next to Booker.
"Dearly beloved we are gathered here today to celebrate one of life's greatest moments, and to cherish the words which shall unit Booker Ivy and Valencia Frost in marriage. Marriage is the promise between two people who love each other, and who trust in love, who honor each other as individuals, and who choose to spend the rest of their lives together." I looked into Booker's eyes and I saw tears rolling down his face as well. "This ceremony will not create a relationship that does not already exist between you. it is a symbol of how far you have come these past few years. It is a symbol of the promises you will make to each other to continue growing stronger as individuals and as partners. No matter the challenges you face, you now face them together, and no matter how much you succeed, you now succeed together. The love between you joins now as one. Who gives this woman in marriage?"
"I do," my father replied.
My father lifted the veil over my face and kissed my cheek and placed my hand inside of bookers and turned to have a seat next to my mother. "Will you please face each other and join hands? Booker, will you take this woman, whose hands you hold, choosing her alone to be your wedded wife? Will you live with her in the state of true matrimony? Will, you love her, comfort her, through good times and bad, in sickness and in health, honor her at all times, and be faithful to her?
"I do."

112

"Valencia, will you take this man, whose hands you hold, choosing him alone to be your wedded husband? Will you live with him in the state of true matrimony? Will, you love him, comfort him, through good times and bad, in sickness and in health, honor him at all times, and be faithful to him?
"I do."
"As you take these preliminary vows, Booker and Valencia, I would have you remember: to love is to come together from the pathways of our past and then move forward...Hand in hand, along the uncharted roads of our future, ready to risk, to dream, and to dare...and always believe that all things are possible with faith and love in God, and in each other. Will you repeat after me? I Booker, take you Valencia, to be my wife, to love and cherish, from this day forward, and thereto pledge you my faith." Booker repeated after the pastor. "I Valencia, take you, Booker, to be my husband, to love and to cherish, from this day forward, and thereto pledge you my faith," I repeated after him. "I understand that you have bought rings as a token of your sincerity?

"Yes, we did."

"Bless O God these rings, that each gives, receives, and wears as a token of the covenant between them and God, and may they ever abide in thy peace, living together in unity, in love, and love, and in happiness, and with good purpose do thy will. Amen."
"Amen"
"Booker, Will you repeat after me: with this ring, I thee wed. Let it ever be to us a symbol of our love." Booker repeated after him. "Valencia, will you repeat after me: With this ring, I thee wed. let it ever be to us a symbol of our love." I repeated after him. "In as much as you, Booker, and you Valencia have consented together in the union of matrimony and you have pledged your faith each the other in the presence of these witnesses, now by the authority vested in me by the state of Missouri, I now pronounce you husband and wife. You may kiss the bride."

Booker gave me the most passionate kiss. We pulled away and turned and looked back at the pastor and he stated, "Ladies and gentleman, I now present to you, Mr. and Mrs. Ivy."

We turned toward everyone, and they were all clapping. The older family members placed the broom down in front of us and we jumped over the broom.

Just thinking back to that day had me so emotional I was ready to hop

on a plane and get out of Kansas City but I have a business to run
just because things aren't going my way I can't just pick up and leave.
I pulled up to the house called a locksmith to come and change my locks.
I walked into my room and began to pull all Bookers clothes out and
shoes basically I pulled all his shit out and I was getting ready to go
Waiting to Exhale on his ass. yall know that part in the movie where
she grabbed all his clothes and everything out the house and placed them
in his car and pulled his car out the garage and burned the car up yea,
I'm thinking about doing that. As I was pulling all of his stuff into the
garage where his other expedition was there was a knock at the
door. Walking over to the door I looked out and it was the locksmith so I
let them in so they could change my locks for me. They began to change
the locks and I sat there on the sectional sofa while they did that. I pulled
out my phone to text my pops.

Me: *hey pops I need a lawyer a good one I'm filing for divorce I
caught booker cheating with his assistant Kelli. They have 2 children and
he has been sleeping with her for 3 years. (Crying emoji)*

Pops: *I got you baby girl I'm making the call now. Are you ok baby
do you need me to come over or anything.*

Me: *I'm ok pops I'm actually changing my locks now and I'm
packing his stuff up in his truck and setting it out for the trash I may just
go waiting to exhale on his ass.*

Pops: *smh daughter well I will check on you later then I love you and
I am here for you.*

Me: *ok dad I love you too.*

After texting my dad, I called my girls up to have them come over so
we can have a girls day and we can trash talk men. I dialed Nora first
she picked up on the first ring.

"What's good Chica?"

"Call the girls."

"Alright, I got you hold on."

She clicked over and call one of the girls and Cora ended up calling
Lora next.

"Ok ladies I need everybody to drop whatever they are doing tonight
and come to the house I need a ladies night real bad and I have to tell
yall what happen today."

"Bihh I am on the way now. The fuck did that fuck boy Booker do
now? Cora loud mouth ass yelled into the phone like I knew she would.

"Just get here and we will talk bring some liquor and I got the food."

I hung up the phone and looked up and the locks smith guy was walking my way so I stood up and walked over to him and he handed me the paper to sign and pay the man for their work.

"Ok Mrs. Ivy could you please sign for your lock change and payment please?"

I signed and gave my payment and handed him his paperwork back and he turned and walked out the door, so I closed and locked the door. So I can finish taking the rest of this nigga stuff to the garage.

One hour later...

The girls were finally all walking through the door, and I was just finishing up cooking baked spaghetti when they all walked in the kitchen and of course, Cora was the loudest of us all when she walks in the building. Grabbing the pan I took it and placed it on the dining table. I walked back in the kitchen and grabbed plates and forks along with glasses and walked back into the dining room and sat the plates, cups, and forks around the table then I took my seat and so did the girls. We all made our own plates and said a silent prayer over our food and dug in. As we all were eating, I decided I may as well go ahead and tell them about the events today.

"Ok ladies I called you all here today because I really needed yall today because after my appointment at the specialist I went to Bookers office to discuss with him that I didn't want to try anymore right now because my heart just isn't in it anymore, I'm tired of losing baby after baby or not even getting pregnant at all. But anyway, I walk into the office and the bitch at the front desk gave me this look like I wasn't supposed to be there today so I walk to his office and I hear moaning not thinking anything of it I'm thinking he watching a porno like he normally does so I just walk into his office and this bitch ass nigga is in there fucking Kelli his assistant over his desk. Not only that this bitch goes on to tell me that they have been fucking for 3 years but they have 2 kids together, so I told him I want a divorce and told him don't bring his ass back to my house. This nigga goes on to tell me we haven't been happy for a long time and he doesn't love me anymore and how he don't know why he let this marriage go on for so long, and I can't give him the one thing that he wants, and that's children and Kelli can. So me being mad he can give 2 fucks about. Then he put me out of his office."

"Bitch I know you got a lick in there or something," Cora asked.

"Bitch don't play me you know I whooped her ass at least up until Carter came and dragged me out his office."

"So, what we need to do? Cause you know I beat that bitch ass I've been and warned that hoe the last we say her to close to Booker ol' community dick ass," Nora ass finally spoke.

Lora spoke up, "Shit you got that nigga shit backed up we can throw that shit in his truck and set that bitch on fire like ol' gurl in Waiting to Exhale did to her husband shit."

I couldn't do anything but laugh cause that's exactly what I plan on doing later. I nodded my head let them know I had already got his shit put in the truck. we finished up our meal and we all went and got ready to burn this nigga shit.

Me: *well I guess you ain't coming for your shit so I'm throwing it out with the trash bye bitch oh yea I'm filing for divorce.*

I put my phone down and began to pull the car out the garage and the ladies had the gas can and poured it all on the inside of the car and I had a match in my hand and lit my cigarette and threw the match at the car and it went up in flames. It was a good thing we didn't have any neighbors. We were the only one on the block. We all walked into the house and went and had our drinks. My phone went off and I looked down and I had a few text messages from this nigga.

Bitch nigga: *you better not touch my shit or imma fuck you up. fuck yo divorce bitch I don't give a fuck I am where I want to be with yo infertile ass.*

Bitch nigga: *oh, so you don't see me texting your ugly black ass*

Bitch nigga: *Aiight bitch I'm on my way then since you want to ignore me.*

Ha-ha, this nigga thought he was scaring somebody, but he didn't put fear in my heart at all. He couldn't get in any way, so I gave no fucks anyway. Plus, I had my gun for safety reasons. I got up and walked in my room to my safe and opened it and grabbed my gun and walked out back into the living room with my girls.

"Ladies so Booker just texted me that he was on his way because I wouldn't reply to him after I told him I was throwing his shit out with the trash."

"Cracking the fuck up and what he thinks he gonna accomplish when he gets her and see his shit burned up," Nora replied.

"Shit I don't know."

CPSIA information can be obtained
at www.ICGtesting.com
Printed in the USA
LVHW021653190319
611166LV00015B/313/P